THE SILENT ROOM

THE SILENT ROOM

Walter Sorrells

DUTTON CHILDREN'S BOOKS

DUTTON CHILDREN'S BOOKS
A division of Penguin Young Readers Group
Published by the Penguin Group
Penguin Group (USA) Inc., 375 Hudson Street, New York, New York 10014, USA
Penguin Group (Canada), 90 Eglinton Avenue East, Suite 700, Toronto, Ontario,
Canada M4P 2Y3 (a division of Pearson Penguin Canada Inc.)
Penguin Books Ltd, 80 Strand, London WC2R 0RL, England
Penguin Ireland, 25 St Stephen's Green, Dublin 2, Ireland (a division of Penguin Books Ltd)
Penguin Group (Australia), 250 Camberwell Road, Camberwell, Victoria 3124, Australia
(a division of Pearson Australia Group Pty Ltd)
Penguin Books India Pvt Ltd, 11 Community Centre, Panchsheel Park, New Delhi—110 017, India
Penguin Group (NZ), Cnr Airborne and Rosedale Roads, Albany, Auckland 1310, New Zealand
(a division of Pearson New Zealand Ltd)
Penguin Books (South Africa) (Pty) Ltd, 24 Sturdee Avenue, Rosebank,
Johannesburg 2196, South Africa
Penguin Books Ltd, Registered Offices: 80 Strand, London WC2R 0RL, England

CIP Data is available.

Published in the United States by Dutton Children's Books,
a division of Penguin Young Readers Group
345 Hudson Street, New York, New York 10014
www.penguin.com/youngreaders

Designed by Irene Vandervoort

Printed in USA   First Edition
10 9 8 7 6 5 4 3 2 1   ISBN 0-525-47697-9

To Caitlin

one

Dear Dad,

Well, the worst finally happened. Mom's new boyfriend moved in with us. His name's Don Guidry. They aren't married yet, so I guess there's still hope.

At nine o'clock this morning he backed this rental truck up to the house and started getting all his stuff out. He always calls me "Sport" and "Champ" and he's going, "Hey, Sport, how about you grab that lamp over there? Hey, Champ, think you could get the other end of that couch?"

He has black leather couches and paintings of sports cars. He made Mom take down the picture you painted of that old barn so he could hang this big photograph of a Ferrari.

And then about noon he started drinking beer and dropping things and cussing a lot. He's real nice to me when Mom's around, but then when she's gone, he's like, "Hey, Sport, you're dragging ass. We need to get this junk in the house pronto, so get off your fat keister."

I'm not fat at all, Dad. He just says stuff like that. He's actually shorter than I am, but he's really strong. He coaches the wrestling team at South Lakes, where I go to high school. That's how Mom met him. He's supposedly the best wrestling coach in Virginia. He was All-American when he wrestled at University of Iowa. I know this because everybody he meets, that's like the first thing out of his mouth, how he was All-American, three years running, and the only reason he didn't go to the Olympics is because the U.S. boycotted the Olympics that year. I hate him, Dad. I know I shouldn't, but I do.

Things are going okay at school. I just started ninth grade. It's kind of weird at the new school. I only know like a third of the kids, and so everybody from all the different middle schools is having to make new friends. All my old friends seem different this year. Duncan McKenzie met this girl named Tracy over the summer and now he eats lunch with her instead of me. She laughs like crazy at all his jokes. Even the dumb ones. I met this guy named Kevin who makes fart noises with his armpit. He seems nice.

Life is weird right now, Dad.

I love you,

Oz

P.S. I wish you weren't dead.

two

Dear Dad,

I don't know what it is about Don Guidry, but I don't like having him in the house. He wears this cologne called Drakkar Noir that I can smell all the time now, even when he's not home.

Yesterday he came home from work and he threw this red cloth thing at me and goes, "Hey, Champ, time for you and me to get down in the basement and train a little."

I was like, "What's this?" Because I thought the thing he threw at me was a girl's bathing suit or something.

He goes, "It's a singlet, you little moron. It's what wrestlers wear."

"It looks like something a girl would wear," I said.

And he goes, "Stop being a faggot." Then Mom came in the room and he mussed up my hair with his hand and grinned like we'd just been making some kind of joke together. "We're going down in the basement and we're gonna work out a little, Rachel," he said.

I looked at Mom and I said, "Uh . . ."

And Mom goes, "Oh, that's nice."

Ever since you died, Dad, Mom has had this look in her eyes like she doesn't have any energy left, like she's trying so hard to feel good about life that she'll grab at anything that makes her feel better—even if it's bogus and nasty. Like Don Guidry. What I'm saying is I could see that if I didn't go down in the basement with Don, she'd feel bad. So I went. Just to make her feel better.

When we got downstairs I said, "Look, Don, just so you know, I'm not going out for the wrestling team or whatever."

He just went, "Put the singlet on."

I said, "I'll wrestle with you if you want, but I'm not putting this on."

And he kind of smiled at me and goes, "Oh, sure you are, Red." Sometimes he calls me Red because of the color of my hair.

And I went, "Oh, no I'm not."

And then he grabbed me and threw me on the ground and started taking my clothes off. He was so strong, I couldn't even stop him and he was lying on top of me and I could smell his Drakkar Noir and finally I just gave up and said, "Okay, I'll put it on."

So I put on the singlet and I felt like a fool. It sagged in the crotch and it was kind of stinky, like some other kid's sweat was in it.

Then Don made me unroll this big rubber mat with a white circle painted on it, and he just started throwing me around. He'd go like, "This is an arm drag," or "This is an over-hook," and then he'd show me some kind of wrestling technique and throw me down and lie on top of me and pin me with all his Drakkar Noir smushing me down into the mat. At first I thought if I didn't fight back, maybe he'd get bored. But he didn't. Eventually I started getting mad, so I tried to stop him from throwing me. But it didn't do any good. He was just smiling and laughing the whole time. And if I tried really hard, fought really hard, then he'd go like, "Come on, you sissy, you can't fight me. You got nothing, Red." Or whatever.

After a while I just wanted to cry. And I guess that was what he was looking for. He got me down in this pin, with my arm all twisted so I felt like I was about to faint and he just held it there. Finally I said, "Please."

"Please what?"

"Please let me go!"

"Please, sir."

"Please, *sir?*"

But he didn't let me go. He just kept my arm all twisted and he lay there on top of me with all his Drakkar Noir and I could feel his breath against my ear and finally he said, "Do you understand what's happening in this house?"

I didn't say anything. I could feel tears in my eyes.

"I asked you a question."

"I don't know," I said.

"Well, let me give you a news bulletin, Sport. I'm here to stay. I'm the man of the house. I don't want to hear a bunch of pansy whining and complaining. Mm-kay? From here on out, it's not gonna be like it was with Mommy, 'I don't feel like cleaning my room,' all that kind of lip and crapola. When I say, 'Jump,' you say, 'How high?' We clear?"

"Please."

"No, that's not the right answer. The right answer is 'Yes, sir.'" Then he twisted my arm a little more.

"Yes, sir."

He cranked it a little more, then let go. Then he got off of me and threw me a towel. "Hit the shower, kid. You stink."

And even though I took a long shower, I smelled like Drakkar Noir all night.

At dinner that night Mom made spaghetti and Don said, "I think Oswald's gonna wrestle at a hundred and thirty-five pounds this year."

"I'm not wrestling," I said.

"Tryouts are at the end of October," Don said. Talking to Mom like I wasn't even there. "We've got a lot of work in front of us, but I think if me and him train every day, he'll be ready by then."

"I'm not wrestling," I said again.

Don pointed at me with his fork. "What did I tell you, Oswald? Huh? About calling me 'Sir'?"

"No," I said.

"Oswald, honey," Mom said.

"Lemme handle this," Don said. Then he grabbed me by my hair and pulled me out of the chair and down the stairs into the basement. When we got down to the bottom of the stairs he said, "You and me are gonna spend a lot of time down here. The sooner you understand who's in charge, the less pain you're gonna feel down here. Got it?"

I just sort of looked at the floor.

He put his face right up in mine like he was trying to look inside my skull. "Got it?"

I shrugged.

That's when he hit me. One big hard slap in the face, so hard that I fell on the ground.

"When you come back up to dinner, you need to say, 'I'm sorry, sir.' Then you can eat."

I sat down there in the basement all night.

The next day Mom said to me, "Why are you being so sullen with Don?"

I didn't say anything.

"He just wants what's best for you," she said.

"No, he doesn't," I said. "He just wants to have you cook his Ore-Ida potatoes and iron his shirts. He doesn't care about me at all."

Mom looked all hurt. "That's not true. You don't know how often we talk about you. He's very . . . concerned."

"About *what*?" I said.

"He thinks you're not . . . doing well."

I squinted at her. "What's that mean? I get all As and Bs. I'm doing fine."

"He says he sees you at school. He says you eat lunch by yourself."

"So?"

"He's concerned, that's all."

"What, he wants me to be some asshole jock and sit at the jock table at lunch and throw food at the geeks and make fun of the kids in the marching band?"

"It's not like that. He says—"

"I don't care what he says!"

"Honey, please," she said. "Don't be disrespectful."

"I'm not calling him sir."

"He comes from a very discipline-oriented background. It would mean a lot to him if you called him sir."

"No."

"It's natural to feel jealous and strange when somebody new comes into your mother's life. I know you miss your father. But Don is here to stay."

"I hate him!"

Mom looked all shocked, and then she started to cry.

I don't know what I'm going to do, Dad. This guy has Mom totally snowed. I have a really bad feeling. Everything smells like Drakkar Noir now. Even Mom. Please help me.

Your son forever,

Oswald

three

Dear Dad,

It just gets worse and worse. Like what happened at the dinner table today.

"Great news!" Don was on his third Miller Lite.

I just sat there. Anything that was great news for Don Guidry was bad news for me. Mom had made steak and Ore-Ida scalloped potatoes, which was Don's favorite meal. Mom was messing with her food, not eating much and looking all nervous.

"Me and your Mom took the plunge this afternoon, Oswald," Don said.

"Huh?"

"The blood test. We went down to the county and took the blood test, got the certificate, the whole nine."

I still didn't have a clue what he was talking about.

"Your mom and me don't want to make a big production, spend a whole bunch of dough on some stupid celebration.

So it'll be just you and me and Mom, a couple of our close friends."

I was still looking at them.

I guess Mom finally figured out that I didn't understand. She reached over and took my hand. That's when I noticed the new ring on her finger. It had this tiny, miserable little diamond on it. One thing I had already learned about Don Guidry was that he was cheap, cheap, cheap. He saved used tinfoil and he gave Mom a huge raft of grief if she didn't use coupons for everything she bought at the store.

"Honey?" Mom said to me. "Don and I are getting married. Next weekend."

Don Guidry gave me the big fake smile that he always used when Mom was in the same room. "You gonna congratulate us? Huh? *Son?*"

Son. Oh, man. Just the sound of that word coming out of his mouth made me want to puke.

"I will never, never, ever be your son," I said. Then I got up and headed for my room.

"Oswald! Oswald, please!" Mom kept calling after me.

"I'll take care of this," Don said.

I got back to my room and slammed the door and locked it. Then I heard Don Guidry's footsteps coming closer and closer. After a minute there was a faint scratching on the door. "Oswald." His voice was quiet and calm. "You're making your mother very unhappy. And when Mommy's unhappy, so is Daddy."

"You're not my dad."

"Wrestling practice after dinner," he said softly. "Seven o'clock sharp."

Seven o'clock came and went. I had put on the loudest, most obnoxious death-metal CD I had, started playing it at full volume. I don't even really like that stuff—but I knew it would piss Don off.

At seven fifteen the door of my room sort of exploded, with bits of wood flying all over the floor. Then Don turned off my stereo and grabbed me by the neck. "Mommy has gone out," he said. "She's very upset and needs to clear her head." Big smile. "So it's just you and me and the good ol' basement."

He dragged me down the stairs. I tried to fight him, but it was no use.

"Get in the singlet," he said.

"No." I was lying in the middle of the wrestling ring.

He picked up the red singlet, threw it at me. I stood up. He hit me, openhanded, knocked me onto the floor. I stood up. He knocked me down. I stood up. He knocked me down. He was smart about it, too, always hitting me in the side of the head where it wouldn't leave a mark on my face that Mom could see.

Finally I stopped getting up.

"You want to know your whole problem, Oswald?" he said. "You're a loser."

"Kiss my ass," I said.

"Nah, see that's the thing. Attitude is something that's reserved for winners. We've been down here working out for, what, like a month? And never once have you made an honest attempt to beat me. Why is that?"

"Maybe because you're a three-time All-American wrestler who can bench-press three hundred pounds?"

"Three-twenty-five, actually," he said. "But that's neither here nor there. Point is, when you're a winner you get to tell other people what to do. But when you're a loser? You say, 'Yes, sir,' and you keep your gay little trap shut. Your problem, Oswald, is you want to *act* like a winner. But you don't have the stones to do what it takes to win."

He stood over me with his Drakkar Noir coming down on me in a cloud.

"Put the singlet on."

I put the singlet on.

After we were done in the basement, we came back upstairs and Mom was sitting in the living room reading a book.

"Oswald has something to say," Don said.

"Congratulations, Mom," I said. "I'm very happy for you and Don."

She looked at me with all that sadness in her eyes and she smiled, and I could see she knew I was just saying it.

For the next week, I tried to beat him. I swear I did, Dad, I really tried. He'd show me all these moves, how to get out of holds and locks and stuff, and then we'd get on the floor and two seconds later he'd be on top of me, whispering into my ear. "Come on, loser, try it again."

I'm getting stronger, Dad. I guess that's a good thing. But there's something else that's happening in me, too. I don't know what it is, but I don't like it.

Love,

Oz

four

Dear Dad,

First thing, I got a D in geometry. I thought I was doing fine, but I guess I wasn't. Mom about stripped a gear when I showed her my report card.

Then on Tuesday in gym class this kid that I know from the Chess Club made some joke about how only a total idiot could get a D in geometry. It was just a little thing, but it made me mad and I grabbed him and knocked him on the floor and put him in this arm lock that Don had showed me. The kid didn't even have a chance.

He was screaming and crying and when the assistant principal and Coach Daniels pulled me off of him, his glasses were broken and all this blood was coming out of his mouth.

That night Mom and Don Guidry sat down with me and Mom said, "What possessed you?"

I just shrugged. I feel like that's all I've been doing lately. Anybody asks me anything, I just look at the floor and shrug.

"Your mother asked you a question," Don said.

"I don't know," I said. "He just pissed me off."

"Three days suspension!" Mom said. "This will go on your permanent record!"

I shrugged again.

Don cleared his throat. "I did my best to get Dr. Robinson to go easy on him. But I can only call in my chips so many times."

"Call in your chips?" Mom looked at Don sharply. "What do you mean?"

Don made this funny face like *Oops!*, then looked at me. I looked back like, *Huh?* I didn't know what he meant either.

"What do you *mean*, Don?" Mom said.

Don sighed loudly, then looked at me like he was really sorry about something. "Sorry, Sport," he said, "but I really have to tell her."

"Tell her what?"

He cleared his throat and shifted around in his chair. "Rachel, look, don't get bent out of shape, but this is actually the third fight he's been in since school started this year."

I could feel my eyes widen.

Mom looked at me accusingly. "Oswald?"

"He's lying!" I said.

Don's voice got harder. "Don't make this worse than it is," he said. Then he gave me a look. I could see what I was in for down in the basement if I didn't go along with him.

"Yes, sir," I said quietly.

"The first time," Don said, "hey, boys will be boys, I didn't think anything of it. The second time, it was a boy who—I'll be honest—I don't like the kid either. So I talked to Dr. Robinson and I made sure that Oswald wouldn't be punished too severely."

"My God," Mom said.

"But this time, he was really pretty, uh—" Don cleared his throat again. "Well, frankly, it was kind of ugly. The kid was kind of a weakling and, well, Oswald knocked out one of his teeth. I'm a little concerned we may have to pay for some dental work."

"Dental work? When were you planning on telling me about this, Oswald?" Mom said.

I shrugged and looked at the floor.

"Go to your room," she said.

"Don't be too hard on him, Rachel," Don said. "He's just having some adjustment problems."

"Go to your *room*," Mom said.

Later, Don and I went down to the basement. Toward the end of our practice, he gave me an opening and I shot in, took him off his feet, put him on his back. It was the first time I'd ever knocked him down. Of course, he immediately reversed me and pinned me. Then he lay there on top of me and said, "You did good up there with your mom. That's why I let you take me down just now."

"Screw you," I said.

I figured he'd twist my arm. But he didn't. He just smiled at me. "You know what I think?" he said. "I think you and me are finally establishing a relationship."

As we were walking up the stairs when we were done, he slapped me on the butt and said, "By the way, I saw you kick

that little geek's ass the other day. Fake arm drag into a fireman's carry! Very nice. Just like I taught you."

I don't know what he's up to, Dad. But why would he lie like
this? He's up to something.
                            Love,
                            Oz

five

Dear Dad,

After I got back from my three-day suspension, I was sitting at a table at lunch and this doper named Leo came over and dropped his tray on the table across from me. Everybody is scared of Leo. I was afraid he was going to steal my cinnamon roll or something, but instead he said, "Three days, huh, Oz?"

I shrugged. "Yeah."

"Heard you uncorked a bottle of whoop-ass on that little pansy."

"Well. You know." I shrugged again. "He pissed me off."

That afternoon Leo came over to the house and we played Xbox and then Leo said, "What's in the fridge, dude?"

"You want something?"

"I'll be back."

He came back out with a couple of glasses of Coke and some cookies and we played Xbox some more.

When Mom came home, he stood up and walked to the door. "I got to go," he said.

"This is Leo, Mom," I said. For some reason I was feeling kind of weird. Mom looked sort of blurry.

I could see her sizing Leo up. He had a tattoo of Chinese writing on the back of his neck and he smelled like dope. Plus there was just something kind of scary-looking in his eyes. It was obvious she didn't like the look of him. And I guess I didn't really blame her.

"Oz! Dude! You didn't tell me your mom was *hot*," he said. Then he winked and pointed his finger at me. "Don't tell her about the you-know-what, bro."

He left, the door banging loudly behind him.

"Don't tell me about *what*?" she said.

"I don't have any idea," I said. Then I stood up and tried to walk across the room to turn off the TV. But for some reason I stumbled and smashed into the coffee table and fell on the floor.

She ran over to see if I was alright. But then when she got close to my face, she got this weird expression on her face. She let go of me and picked up the glass that my Coke was in and sniffed it.

"Is there vodka in here?" She took a sip of my Coke. "My God, there's *vodka* in here!"

Which I guess explained why I was feeling so weird.

"Leo must have slipped it in there," I said. "I didn't know anything about—"

"Stop!" she shouted. "Just stop lying to me! What is happening to you?"

. . .

The next day when I got off the bus, Mom was home from work early, standing in the driveway.

"What's going on, Mom?" I said.

"Please get in the car," Mom said.

"What for?" I said.

"Just get in the car."

"You're acting weird, Mom," I said.

"In the car."

I got in and we drove over to this little office park near the mall in Reston and Mom had this grim expression on her face the whole time. Down toward the end of the cheesy little office park—between a Tae Kwon Do school and a transmission repair shop—was a tiny office with a sign over the door that said:

MILTON CHILDERS, B.ED.

CERTIFIED COUNSELOR

SPECIALIST IN DISTURBED CHILDREN

Disturbed children! I got in one fight and I made a D in geometry. That hardly made me a disturbed child.

We went into the waiting room. There was indoor-outdoor carpeting on the floor, and all the furniture looked like it had been bought at a flea market.

After a minute a thin little guy with a sour expression on his face poked his head out the door and said, "Oswald Turner."

I nodded. "Come on in." Mom started to stand up, but he pointed at her chair and said, "Mom, you stay out here." I didn't like the way he talked to her. Like she was his waitress or something. Mom sat back down.

I followed the sour little guy back into his office. As he was closing the door, I slumped down in a chair across from the cheap fake wood desk with the Naugahyde office chair behind it.

He sat down, looked at me for a long time. There was a sign on the wall that said: CAN'T with a big diagonal red stripe through it.

"Let me ask you a question, kiddo," he said finally. His voice was conversational. "Did I instruct you to sit down?"

"Uh . . ."

"*Uhhhhhhhh* no I did not. Stand your butt up!"

I stood slowly up.

"Stand at attention. Show a little pride here for Christ's sake. Shoulders back, chin up."

He kept staring at me as I straightened up. Finally he nodded.

"Good. Now see there's a lot of counselors out there that are all, *Oh, gosh and golly tell me about all your problems and your bed-wetting and how sad you are about your cat dying* and all that shit. Huh-uh, son. Not me. I'm a behaviorist. Do you know what that means?"

I shook my head.

"I figured not. Behaviorism. It's a psychological term for a theory of the human personality. Basic idea is: you are what you do." He stared at me some more like he had just dropped all kind of wisdom on me and now he was letting it sink in. "You are. What you do."

I nodded.

"Now your mom came in here for a preadmittal meeting and she told me about how your dad died three years ago and all about his agonizing death from cancer, and how you and him used to go camping together, and how you helped him fix up old cars in his machine shop, and how crazy you were about your old man and, well, frankly I kind of dozed off about halfway through this litany of sadness and excuses. Mm-kay?"

I nodded.

Mr. Childers's eyes narrowed. "'Yes, *sir*,' I believe is the phrase you were searching for, *Oswald*." Every time he said my name, he gave it this sarcastic little emphasis. Just like Don always did.

"Huh?" I said.

He was wearing one of those big college rings with the red stone on it. He turned the stone around so it was on the inside of his finger, making a big show of it. Then he stood, came around the desk and popped me in the back of the head. Man, that ring stung like crazy! I had all these funny colors running around in front of my eyes for a second.

"I can't hear you," he said.

"Yes, sir," I whispered.

"Good. Now you get the picture. See, *Oswald*, I'm not one of these namby-pamby I-care-how-you-feel type counselors. Frankly? I don't give a hoot if you feel sad because your dad died an agonizing death. Things like that happen. It's not right, it's not fair, but they do. And that's no excuse for being a loser."

"Yes, sir," I said.

"Now drop down and give me fifty push-ups."

Mr. Childers went back and sat behind the desk while I started doing the push-ups. I got to about fifteen and he said, "Start over and count them out loud."

"One . . . two . . . three . . . four . . ." At about twelve, my arms kind of gave out.

"Keep going," he said.

"I can't," I said.

"Oh! Oh!" he said. "No! No! No, you didn't!"

I just lay there.

"Did I just hear you say, 'I can't'?"

"I'm sorry, I . . ."

"Stand up!"

I stood up.

He pointed at the sign on the wall, CAN'T with the big red stripe through it. "What does that mean?"

"Uh . . . I guess it means you don't like people saying they can't do stuff."

"I don't like people saying they can't do stuff . . . *sir*."

"Sir," I said.

"So then I guess when I tell you to do fifty push-ups and you do like, five, and then whine like a girl about how you can't? What? Would that maybe piss me off?"

"Uh . . ."

"Get your ass on the floor, *Oswald*, and snap out fifty."

I got on the floor. There were all these dust bunnies and toenail clippings on the floor under his desk. I started doing the push-ups. When I got to twenty-two, I just gave out.

Mr. Childers got up and put his foot on my neck. "I'm standing here with my foot on your neck until you give me fifty. Clear?" he said.

"Yes, sir."

I did a few more, gave out, did a few more, gave out, did a few more. Every time I'd do one or two, he'd press down with his foot and slam me into the floor. It took me about half an hour, staring at the toenails and lint, before I got to fifty.

When I was done he said, "I think we're making terrific progress here." Talking in this real sarcastic voice. "See you next week!"

"How'd it go?" Mom said.

"Fine," I said.

We rode for a while. I wanted to cry. But a few months after you died, Dad, I decided that I would never cry again, not in my whole life. I had cried every night for a long time, and finally I just got sick of feeling like a baby.

"Can I please, please, please, please never go back there?" I said finally.

"Your stepfather said Mr. Childers has great insight into the teenage mind."

"Could you not use his name in the same sentence as the word 'father'?" I said. "My father would never send me to a guy like that."

"I know Don is not your blood father. But he's been nothing but kind to you. Look how much time he's devoted to helping with your wrestling."

"Sh'yeah!" I said.

Mom gave me a look.

"What!" she said. "Tell me, what has he ever done to you?"

I felt this horrible tightness in my chest, like I was trapped in a tiny box that would never open. "I think I'm gonna kill myself," I said.

Mom slammed on the brakes. "What did you just say?"

I smiled weakly. "Hey, I'm just kidding! God!"

"Oswald, you're scaring me," she said finally.

"Well, I am a disturbed child," I said. "I guess you should be scared."

She kept driving. And her lip was quivering.

It never used to be like this, Dad. Why has everything changed?

Love,

Oz

six

Dear Dad,

Every week I went to see Mr. Childers. Each time it was the same routine. He didn't talk to me about my feelings or how I was doing in school or any of the stuff that therapists always do on TV. It was just push-ups, push-ups, push-ups. So I practiced push-ups every day, and started lifting some weights that Don kept down in the basement. By the third meeting I could snap out fifty without even breaking a sweat. After a few weeks I looked in the mirror and I was amazed at all these little muscles in the back of my arms that I'd never seen before. Blue veins were popping up on my pale skin.

But it didn't matter. Mr. Childers didn't really care. If I did fifty push-ups, he wanted a hundred. If I did a hundred, he wanted two hundred and fifty. By the third meeting, he had stopped hitting me with his ring and putting his foot on my neck. He just sat there reading *Maxim* with his feet on the desk, telling me to do more. After the fourth meeting, he called my mom in and they talked for a long time while I sat in the waiting room.

We drove home and Mom had tears running down her face and had to pull the car off to the side of the road.

"What?" I said.

"Do you really hate me that much?" she said finally.

"I don't hate you!" I said.

"Mr. Childers said you told him that you wrote a story for English class about a boy named Oswald who killed his mother and ate her."

"I never told him that!"

She took a long, slow breath. "Oswald . . ." She reached over and put her hand on mine. "I feel like I'm losing you."

"Wonder why," I said sarcastically.

"What's that supposed to mean?"

But I didn't say anything. Truth was, I knew that I was screwed now. I was totally, completely hosed. And there was nothing I could do about it.

"You think this is about Don?" she said. "This is not about Don. Don loves you. This is about *you*."

I felt this giant weight pressing down on me. If I said anything to her, if I said that Don was running some kind of game on her, then she'd just think I was lying or being paranoid.

"Forget it," I said.

"You need to start being honest. Mr. Childers tells me that you lie to him constantly."

"Look, whatever. I don't want to talk about it."

.   .   .

When we got home, I went into my room and put on some loud music and didn't come out for supper, even when Don came and banged on the door.

I'm really scared, Dad.

Your son,

Oz

seven

Dear Dad,

Remember how a while back I said that the worst had finally happened? I was *so* wrong. Things just keep getting worse. Today when I got home from school, Mom was standing in the living room with these little red spots on each cheekbone. She was holding something out toward me.

"How come you're not at work?" I said.

"Would you care to explain this, Oswald?" she said.

"What?"

She waggled the thing in her hand. It was a small plastic bag. "I found this in your room. With the porno DVDs, by the way."

"You were in my room?" I said. I grabbed the little bag out of her hand. It was pot. I threw it on the floor. "This is not mine. I don't smoke that stuff."

Mom's face was all hard. "Stop. Lying. To. Me."

"I do not keep pot in my room. Or pornos, for that matter. If you found them there, it's because Don planted them there."

"Stop!" Her voice cracked.

"I'm warning you—" I said. I was about to say, *I'm warning you. Don's going to do something bad pretty soon.* But she didn't give me a chance.

"Oz!" Mom flinched like I was about to hit her.

"What? Are you afraid I'm gonna kill you and eat you? God!" I went back to my room and slammed the door.

"Things are going to change!" my mother yelled.

I put on my headphones, cranked up the tunes, and then I couldn't hear her yelling anymore.

Love,

Oz

eight

Dear Dad,

Well, good news. The suspense is finally over. I knew that something was coming. And, boy, did it suck. But at least now I know what Don was up to.

It happened at two o'clock in the morning. I was lying in bed sleeping and suddenly something woke me up. It was somebody calling my name.

"Oswald! Oswald! Let's go, bud. Time to wake up!"

At first I thought it was Don, but then when I finally woke and sat up in bed, all I could see was a flashlight shining in my eyes. I could tell that it wasn't Don, though, because the guy holding the flashlight was too big to be Don.

For a second I thought it was a home invasion or something, and my heart started pounding, and I about peed in my pants.

"Wake up!" the man said.

"What!" I said. "Who are you?"

"My name's Mr. Edson. You're coming with me."

It all just seemed totally weird and whacked and I couldn't figure out what he was talking about.

"Huh? What are—?"

"I'll answer your questions later." The man standing over me had a real firm voice. Not mean, necessarily, but hard. Like a cop. "Right now you need to get up and put your clothes on."

"Mom!" I yelled. "Don!"

"Mr. and Mrs. Guidry are downstairs in the living room," he said. "Now, get up and put your clothes on."

"No!" I said.

"There's two ways to do this," he said. "The easy way and the hard way. The easy way, you cooperate. The hard way? I cuff you and you come outside in your underwear. Now which one is it going to be?"

He sounded totally reasonable and calm. And now that my eyes had adjusted to the glare of the flashlight, I could see him better. He was about six foot three and looked like he'd played football when he was young.

I felt like I was in some kind of horrible dream and I couldn't wake up. I got out of bed, put on my pants and a shirt and some sneakers.

"Good job, Oswald. You're doing good," Mr. Edson said. "Now let's go."

He took my arm and walked me down the stairs. I saw a glimpse of Don and Mom in the living room. Don was holding Mom's hand and Mom was crying.

"Mom!" I yelled.

"It's for your own good, Oswald," she mumbled. But she didn't look at me.

"Mom, please! What's going on here?"

She didn't answer.

Mr. Edson kind of yanked me out of the room and through the front door. "This is the hardest part," he said. "After this, it gets easier. Trust me on this."

I followed him in a daze. There was a Ford Crown Victoria—the kind of car police drive—sitting at the curb with the motor running. It had been cheaply repainted, so you could still see the insignia of a shield on the door, still halfway showing through the white paint.

"Backseat," Mr. Edson said. He put his hand on my head and pushed me into the backseat the way they always do on that show *Cops.*

I kept staring at the house as he closed the door, thinking Mom would come out and do something. But she never did.

Mr. Edson got in the front seat, dropped the car into gear, and started driving. After a minute he turned the radio on to an oldies station. They played this song called "Sittin' on the Dock of the Bay" about this guy sitting by the ocean, watching the water. It seemed like the saddest song in the world. Toward the end of the song the singer started whistling the tune. Mr. Edson whistled through his teeth along with the music, slightly out of key. Outside it was very dark and the lights in most of the houses were off. I imagined everybody inside lying there sleeping without any worries or anything, and I just wanted to cry. But I couldn't do it.

I miss you so much, Dad. Why did you have to die? Are there any reasons why things happen or is the world just like a big mess that's designed to make everybody miserable? I wish I had an answer to this.

"Where are we going?" I said finally.

"Your parents have placed you in a school," he said. "It's called the Briarwood School. It's a boarding school down in Georgia that specializes in educating kids like you, boys who've been in some trouble and need a solid, disciplined environment where they can engage in some attitude adjustment."

I sighed loudly.

"I'm gonna tell you something," Mr. Edson said. "I'm what's known as a transporter. This is my whole job, picking up young individuals such as yourself and transporting them to schools like Briarwood. I'll tell you honestly—Briarwood is not a picnic. I've got six or eight schools as clients and some of the schools are tougher, some are softer. But, hey, it is what it is. These people that run these schools, whatever you may think, they have your best interests at heart."

I sat there watching the houses go by.

"Son, being your age is hard. I know this. I was wild when I was your age. But what I eventually found out is, if you make a decision to suck it up and stop complaining, stop fighting the world—then the world will stop fighting you. You keep banging your head against the world, you know what you get?"

I shrugged.

"A headache."

Thank you for that, I thought. The funny thing was, though, I could see he was being sincere about what he said. The guy didn't seem like a jerk. He was just doing his job, probably thought he was doing me a favor.

"You can lie down back there, get some sleep," he said. "The school is about a twelve-hour drive from here."

"How do you get a job like this?" I said.

"I used to be a cop. Retired as a homicide detective about four years ago. I like this job because I know I'm helping boys in trouble. Trust me on this. You go down there to Briarwood, work the program, do what they say, you'll find all that anger and fear starting to go away. I promise you. And when you go back home, it'll be like night and day."

"How long will I be there?"

He shook his head. "I guess that depends on you, son."

I lay down, listened to the wheels humming and thumping against the road. I never slept, not once. I felt like the whole world went dark when you died, Dad. But it never felt quite as dark as it did tonight.

> Love,
> Your son forever and ever,
> Oz

nine

Dear Dad,

Well, I'm here. The Briarwood School.

Do you remember this kid named Jason Brentwell who I went to elementary school with? Well, a couple of years ago his parents sent him to this boarding school up in Connecticut. He came back with pictures of his school, and there were all these really cool old buildings with ivy on the sides and these kids wearing neckties and blue jackets, and they were on a river where all these kids were rowing these long, skinny boats and stuff.

Well, the Briarwood School is nothing like that.

The sun came up and we drove through Atlanta and then kept going south. Georgia must be a lot bigger than I thought, because it seemed like we drove forever, going south and south and south. After three or four hours of driving south, we turned off the big interstate highway onto this little podunk two-lane road that went dead straight through a bunch of pine trees. We drove for another hour or so, going through these little crappy towns that looked like they'd dried up about fifty years ago. And then we got into this swampy area, with greenish brown water in the ditches beside the road and pine forests that seemed to go on forever and ever.

Finally we turned onto a smaller road and then a smaller road and then there were hardly any cars at all. Sometimes there was Spanish moss hanging from the trees like the beards of old dead men, and once I saw an alligator lying in a ditch. It was chewing on some kind of big white bird, and the bird's claw was sticking out of the alligator's mouth.

"Gators got hunted almost to extinction about a hundred years ago," Mr. Edson said. "But they put them on the protected list and now you can't go through this area without practically tripping over them."

"Really?"

"Couple years back a fellow down in Florida killed one that weighed over a thousand pounds. A gator that big could take down a small cow without breaking a sweat."

I looked out at the swampy areas going off into the woods. "What is this place?" I said.

"You ever seen a map that has a big white spot on it?" Mr. Edson said. "One of those places where there's nothing? No people, no roads, no houses, no farms, no factories, no nothing? Well, that's what this is. It's a white spot on the map of the world. Not many places left like this in the US of A."

As he said that, we passed this sign on the road that said, WELCOME TO PILGREEN COUNTY. Only, some of the letters were gone because they'd been shot out with a shotgun, and the letters that were there were faded and peeling. And the sign itself had fallen over sideways. There was some kind of dead animal in the road, with a big smear of blood next to it and flies swarming on the corpse, and the second we passed it, there was this horrible smell in the car.

"We're right on the edge of the Okefenokee Swamp," Mr. Edson said. "We'll be there soon."

And sure enough, about five minutes later there was a big stone pillar on the side of the road capped by a brass plaque with the name of the school on it. It looked okay—like the entrance to a nice subdivision in Reston or Great Falls.

We turned onto the road past the sign. Within about a hundred feet the blacktop disappeared and the road turned into a rutted, sandy track covered with crushed seashells. I figured we'd be there in about thirty seconds. But instead we kept driving for another five minutes or so, a cloud of dust coming up behind us as Mr. Edson threaded his way down the twisting little road.

Finally we stopped. I didn't see anything that looked like a school.

Mr. Edson got out of the car and came around to open my door. It was a really creepy place, with these live oak trees covered with Spanish moss and this smell like everything was rotting around us. In front of us was a flat expanse of lake. For a second I had this feeling like maybe he was going to just take me out of the car and shoot me. Or maybe something even worse.

But just as I was about to get all panicky, a figure moved in front of us.

"How you doing, Mr. Pardee?" Mr. Edson said.

The man in front of us said nothing. He was an old guy wearing overalls, a white T-shirt, and a green camouflage baseball cap that looked like he had been using it to wipe the oil off car-engine dipsticks for about forty years. There was something vaguely menacing about him—though I couldn't tell you exactly what it was. Just an expression in his eyes, like he was looking straight through you. He cocked his head at us, indicating we should follow him, then he began walking away.

"We go from here on an airboat," Mr. Edson said. "The school is on an island. There's no road out to the school. Only way in or out is by boat."

We followed the old guy in the overalls down to the edge of the lake, eventually coming to one of those airboats like they have in the Everglades in Florida. In front were some seats bolted on top of two aluminum pontoons. In the back was a big car engine attached to a huge airplane propeller blade.

The old guy unlocked a metal box on the dashboard of the airboat with a set of keys hanging from a chain attached to his belt, then fired up the motor. It made a horrendous noise.

"Watch that propeller," Mr. Edson said. "There's a cage around it, but if you get your hand through there, it'll cut it slap off."

We climbed onto the machine and the old man began steering the boat across the water. If this hadn't been the second crappiest day of my life, it would have been really cool. We went tearing through the swamp, under huge trees covered with Spanish moss, down little inlets where the vegetation was so close you could touch it, past cypress knees that stuck up from the black water. One time I saw a huge gator swimming lazily through the water. Another time I saw a snake hanging from a tree.

"Water moccasin!" Mr. Edson yelled, pointing at it. I could barely hear him over the roar of the engine. "Extremely poisonous!"

It must have taken us fifteen or twenty minutes of threading our way through the swamp before we finally slowed down. On the shore in front of us was a sort of boathouse with a big door made of galvanized steel coming down into the water. The old guy pulled out a remote control for a garage-door opener and the big bay door slowly opened in front of us. He piloted the boat into the boathouse, killed the engine, closed the big steel door behind us.

When the airboat motor stopped, the whole world seemed to have gone silent.

"We just crossed five miles of gator-infested swamp," Mr. Edson said. "Even if you knew the way, you'd drown or get bitten to death by snakes out here. So don't get clever and think about trying to wander out here by yourself."

"Sure," I said.

We got off the boat and walked up a small path and out into a clearing.

Mr. Edson waved his hand. "Behold, the Briarwood School."

I don't know what I'd expected. But not this. In front of us was a cheap-looking, ramshackle building mostly made of white-painted cinder blocks. Some parts looked fairly new and some must have been twenty or thirty years old. Some parts had a red metal roof; some were roofed with tar paper. It didn't look like there had been any plan. It was all drab, functional, slapdash, and cheap-looking.

"It used to be owned by the army," Mr. Edson said. "They did some kind of research on nuclear bombs down here. The Briarwood School bought it a few years back. It's still a little, ah, rustic."

I surveyed the area. A group of kids wearing white T-shirts and blue jeans was running past us in a military formation, yelling something in unison. They didn't seem gung ho, though, like army guys on TV always did. They just looked sweaty and dispirited and tired and beat down. I noticed one fat kid lagging behind. He had tears running down his face, and this drill-sergeant-looking guy with a buzz cut and big muscles was yelling at him, calling him a girl and a crybaby and all this stuff.

We got onto a golf cart and the old guy drove us toward the ramshackle building. Instead of stopping there, though, the golf cart kept on going. On the other side of the big building was a maintenance shed with a rusted tractor parked out front. We passed it, and there in front of us was a large, grim three-story stone house.

"That's Dr. Kinnear's house," Mr. Edson said.

"Who's Dr. Kinnear?"

"He's the headmaster."

"The what?"

"It's like a principal. The director of the school."

"Oh."

"A real visionary. He has an amazing understanding of the psychology of kids in your situation. I met him once. Extraordinary man. Unfortunately his health's not so good right now, so you may not see a lot of him around the school."

We drove past the headmaster's house and up to another stone building. This one said ADMINISTRATION on the front. This and the headmaster's house were the only buildings on the campus that looked halfway decent—sort of like cheap imitations of the buildings at that school in Connecticut that my friend Jason Brentwell went to.

The creepy old guy pulled the golf cart up to the curb and stopped. Mr. Edson didn't get out. "Nobody *wants* to be here, son," he said. "But that doesn't mean it's a bad place. Sometimes you have to go through bad things in life to learn what's good and what's not."

I just sat there looking around.

"Me, I spent four years in the army. Turned me around completely. Did I like being a buck private with some big redneck sergeant yelling at me all the time? Shoot, no. But I served my time and somewhere along the way I learned that life doesn't give anybody a free ride. You do your time here, do what they say, you'll come out the other side a strong, disciplined young man. I sometimes wish I'd been sent to a place like this."

"No, you don't," I said.

Suddenly he was all business. "You'll notice," he said, "there's no wall around this place. Why? Because—like I said— we're in a white spot on the map. There's no place to go. In a thirty-mile circle there's not a town, not a phone booth, not a cell-phone tower, not a boat landing, not a house. It's just miles and miles of pine trees and swamps and alligators. You do *not* want to get lost out there. Trust me."

I shrugged.

"So. You gonna run?"

I shook my head.

"Good. 'Cause I hate putting boys in cuffs when I deliver them."

We both stood up. The sun and the heat hit me in a wave.

"Come with me," he said.

I don't know why, but despite everything he'd said about the white spot on the map and the alligators and how it was impossible to find your way through the swamp and everything, I just had this terrible feeling about being here and suddenly I had this thought like maybe I could run away and swim back to the road and hitch a ride and get back to Virginia. And then I could explain to Mom what had happened and how stupid she was for buying Don's lies and she'd make him go away and everything would be fine again.

And so, without even really planning it, I just started running.

"Nah, kid," Mr. Edson yelled. "You don't want to start this way!" He sounded almost sad about it.

I ran past the stone house and past the maintenance shed. Then I heard this loud noise, kind of like a siren going off. I came around the other side of the big ramshackle building and there were all the kids lined up like soldiers. When they saw me running, they started laughing and yelling. "The new kid's bailing!" one boy yelled. And then everybody else started pointing and laughing and joining in. "Check it out! The new kid's bailing! The new kid's bailing!"

Then I heard another noise. Dogs.

I couldn't tell how many of them there were. But there were a bunch.

"*Oh* hell!" the kids were yelling. "Here come the dogs!"

I had planned to head straight back down the gravel road, but now that I heard these dogs, I decided to make a break for the woods which encircled the campus like a dark noose. I looked back and the kids were laughing and jumping up and down, and the muscular guy was yelling at them to shut up, and then there were these black streaks coming around the side of the building.

Dobermans. Four of them. Teeth bared, muscular bodies straining.

They headed straight for me.

I hit the woods, looked for someplace to hide. But there was nothing. I was pounding along on this spongy ground and the trees were all planted in rows like corn so it seemed like you could see for miles down each row of trees. The tops of the trees had all grown together, blotting out the light. I felt like I was in some weird maze in a science-fiction movie.

I looked back and the dogs were streaking toward me and there was just no place, no place, no place to go.

I jumped onto a tree, started shinnying my way painfully up the trunk. There were no branches, nothing to hold onto. But I was so scared, I managed to get about ten feet up the tree by the time the dogs got to me. They surrounded me, barking and howling and gnashing their teeth, whirling around and jumping up toward my feet. Their claws were clicking and scratching on the bark of the tree. I knew if I came down, they could kill me in about a second. I looked up. The top of the tree was forty feet above me and my arms were weakening. No way I'd make it to the top.

Finally I just closed my eyes and hung on, waiting for my strength to fail.

That's when I thought of you, Dad. Back when you were dying, you used to ask me to come into your room and you had all these tubes in your arms and then you'd talk to me, tell me things. You'd say, "Son, this is really important. Remember this." And your eyes were all wet and swimmy and you'd tell me something that I was supposed to remember.

But you know what, Dad? I couldn't remember any of it. I couldn't remember anything you said. And I felt like, maybe, if I'd really listened, if I'd paid attention to what you'd said, I wouldn't have been in this place.

Suddenly—just as my arms were about to give out—the dogs went quiet. I opened my eyes.

Standing there below me was the old man in overalls. He had a pipe in his mouth that was carved in some kind of design that I couldn't make out, and there was smoke coming up around his head. In his hand, he had a short leather strap. The dogs were all sitting now, perfectly motionless, their black eyes fixed on my face. They might as well have been statues.

"Get out that tree, boy," he said quietly.

I was starting to slip. The bark was cutting my arms and my hands.

"I told you, get out that tree."

He came up and grabbed my shoe, yanked. I fell on the ground with a sickening thump. It knocked the breath out of me. All I could do was make this wheezing noise.

"Get up," the old man said.

I stood up slowly, wheezing. One of the dogs twitched, like

it was going to make a move toward me. The old man's arm flicked out lazily and the leather strap bit into the dog's flank. It didn't even whimper. But after a minute, a small trail of blood began to ooze out of its fur.

"Learn from these dogs, boy," the old man said. "Except Sissy, the one I just whipped, they all do exactly what I tell 'em. You be like those three, you gonna be fine here. But you be like Sissy here, you gonna pay the price."

He turned and started walking away from me, back toward the school, the rank smell of his pipe trailing after him. I followed. The dogs made a little circle around me and we began walking toward the light.

A few minutes later we got back to the stone administration building. Mr. Edson was leaning against the wall, shaking his head. "I'm gonna have to cuff you now," he said gruffly. He slapped the cuffs on me, the cool metal biting into my skin. "I thought you were smarter."

Then he grabbed me and pushed me in front of him, through the large oak doors and into a dim hallway. We walked down the hallway and into a small white room.

"This is Mrs. Kinnear," Mr. Edson said. "Mrs. Kinnear is the school administrator. She's also married to Dr. Kinnear, the headmaster of the school who I was telling you about."

An extremely beautiful woman with glossy black hair was sitting behind a large desk made of some kind of fancy wood. My guess was that she was in her late thirties. Mr. Edson walked up to the desk, put a piece of paper on it. Mrs. Kinnear signed the paper and Mr. Edson took off my cuffs and left.

Without looking up from the desk, Mrs. Kinnear said, "Take off your shoes."

"Excuse me?"

"Take off your shoes."

"Why?"

For the first time, she looked up at me. Her eyes were a deep green. "Young man," she said. "At the Briarwood School, we have thirty-seven Rules of Behavior. Rule One: Questions are disrespectful. Rule Two: Refer to all adults as sir or ma'am." She paused. "Now, take off your shoes."

I sighed loudly. Then I took off my shoes.

"What I see," she said, "is a young man with no self-respect. Self-respect is a reflection of the respect you offer others. This is the lesson you will learn here. This is the central insight into human behavior and psychology offered by Dr. Kinnear."

"I'm not even supposed to *be* here," I said.

She pursed her lips. "Please do not offer your opinion. Your opinion is not needed at the Briarwood School. Furthermore, when I speak, please signify your interest in what I'm saying by answering, 'Yes, ma'am.'"

"Yes, ma'am."

"If you do not say sir or ma'am to a member of the staff here, it will be considered a DR."

"DR? Ma'am?"

"DR stands for 'disrespect.' Any and all disrespectful acts you commit here will be assessed to you in the form of DR points. Get too many DR points, you lose privileges." She studied me with her glistening green eyes. "Take off your belt."

"Yes, ma'am." I took off my belt.

"Place it on the floor next to you."

"Yes, ma'am." I put my belt on top of my shoes.

"Go out the door, turn left, walk to the end of the hallway. You'll find a room with your name on the door. Enter the room. On the desk in the room you will find a printed list of the thirty-seven rules. You will stay in that room until you can recite the thirty-seven rules, word for word, in correct order."

"You want me to go now?"

"Now, what?"

"Now . . . uh . . . *ma'am?*" I was used to that sort of question from Don Guidry, so I knew what she was getting at.

"Now."

I wanted to know why I couldn't take my belt or my shoes. "May I ask a question, ma'am?"

"No, you may not."

I wanted to strangle her. But what was I going to do? I clamped my jaw shut, left my shoes, and walked silently down the hallway, holding my pants up so that they wouldn't fall down.

My name was written—misspelled "Ozwald"—in black Magic Marker on a piece of paper taped to the door. I walked in, found myself in a tiny, stifling, windowless room. There was a bed with no sheets on it against one wall, and a desk against the other.

In the center of the desk was a sheet of paper, badly photocopied, that said

BRIARWOOD SCHOOL RULES OF BEHAVIOR
by William F. X. Kinnear, IV, Ph.D.

I sat in the chair for a while. After about ten minutes I heard some footsteps coming down the hallway. I figured somebody would come talk to me, but all that happened was that a key turned in the lock. I could hear the bolt clicking shut. That's when I noticed that the door had no handle or knob. I was locked in. I waited for the footsteps to go away, then I banged on the door once, just to see how strong it felt. It was solid, heavy wood. It might as well have been made of steel.

I sat down and started reading.

RULE ONE. QUESTIONS ARE DISRE-SPECTFUL. DO NOT ASK QUESTIONS.

That's when I remembered something. Dad, ever since the moment I got treed by the dogs, I had been having this sick, terrible feeling in my stomach because I couldn't remember any of the things you'd said to me back when you were dying. But suddenly I remembered one of them.

"Remember this, son," you'd said to me. "Question everything."

It hit me in a flash. I could see everything in the hospital room. The little machine they had you hooked up to and the swimmy look in your eyes and the crappy little gown you wore and the red color of your hair, which is the exact same color as mine. I wonder if you felt as bad then as I do now? I bet you did. I bet it really sucks dying, huh?

What am I supposed to do? Dad, if I do like you told me to and I question everything, it's going to be like that old man with the dogs said. It's going to be bad for me.

What am I supposed to do?

Love,

Oz

ten

Dear Dad,

Memorizing is not my strong suit. I'm really good at puzzles and word problems and remembering stuff about history. I'm really good at reading comprehension. But memorizing poetry and French verbs and stuff like that—I totally suck at it.

I have been in the room for a long time now. Five days, I think. Or maybe six. Every day this old lady named Mrs. Ellis comes in and gives me a tray of food. The food is the same every day. For breakfast I get these slimy powdered eggs and cold toast and orange juice and bacon that's either burned or barely cooked. There's no lunch. By suppertime, I'm starving. Supper is a baloney sandwich with bread that's starting to dry and curl up, green beans, mashed potatoes with gravy, a greasy biscuit, and either banana pudding or Jell-O with canned fruit in it.

After I eat, Mrs. Kinnear sometimes comes in. She makes me stand at attention, then she tells me to recite the rules. I've been studying them for almost a week, but still I always stumble somewhere along the way. She tells me that I'm not trying hard enough. Then she goes out and locks the door. I think if she weren't a lady, I would have hit her with the food tray by now. A while after I eat supper, the light goes out and the room is totally dark.

She let me have a shower once. But now I'm getting kind of stinky again.

There's no radio, no TV, and the only book in the room is the Bible. I found a pen hidden under the bed, so I'm writing this in little tiny letters on the back of the paper with the thirty-seven rules on it. If I run out of paper, I don't know what I'll do.

Mostly I do push-ups and I run in place and I study the thirty-seven rules. Also I read the Bible. I'm at this part where they're telling about all the people who begat this guy who begat this guy who begat this guy. I hope it gets more exciting after a while.

I did 537 push-ups today. My arms are really sore.

In the middle of the night I heard a sound in the hallway. Somebody scratching lightly on the door. Then a whisper.

"Dude! Dude!"

I could see a shadow against the light that came in at the bottom of the door. "Who is it?" I said.

"My name's Sean."

"Oz," I said.

"Oz? Like yellow-brick-road Oz?"

"Short for Oswald."

"Oh. Yeah, I could see how you'd need a nickname. So, what did you do to end up here?"

"Nothing."

"Me neither," the boy on the other side of the door whispered. Then he kind of snickered. "You holding up okay?"

"I guess."

"Did they take your shoes and your belt?"

"Yeah."

"The last kid in here hung himself by his shoelaces, dude."

"Did he die?"

"What, are you a retard? Of course he died."

"I can't get these rules memorized."

"Hey, the rules are nothing. They're just showing you who's boss because you tried to run away. That totally rocked, by the way. They haven't put the dogs on anybody for like six months."

"I thought I was gonna get killed."

"They're like specially trained takedown dogs. They don't kill you; they just grab you and pull you down and hold you. Their teeth are filed down so you don't get any major wounds." The kid on the other side of the door laughed. "Still, I bet it hurts like crazy, huh?"

I heard something slide under the door.

"What's that?" I said.

"Pop-Tart. Hang in there, dude."

Then I heard footsteps as the boy tiptoed away. I scrabbled around on the floor, found the Pop-Tart, wiped the dust off it, and ate it. It was strawberry, and it was the best Pop-Tart ever made in the history of the universe.

So maybe there's hope after all. I've got to get these stupid rules memorized. I don't want to go crazy and kill myself like that other kid.

> Love,
> Oz

eleven

Dear Dad,

Well, I'm out.

I did the thirty-seven rules this morning to Mrs. Kinnear and messed up a little once. She rolled her eyes like, *Here we go again with the moron*, then went away.

But then five minutes later the door opened and this guy who said he was the dean of students told me I was being allowed out of what he called the "intake chamber." Which sounds like part of a toilet or something. He took me down to his office and talked to me. It seems like he's basically the same as a guidance counselor, but with a fancy title. His name is Mr. Akempis.

Mr. Akempis was a sort of wimpy-seeming little guy with thin, blond hair and polyester pants that were pulled up a little too high and a look on his face like he'd just bitten down on a rotten pickle.

"Mm-kay," he said, "please have a seat, Oswald." He had a

high voice like he was talking out of his nose and he blinked a lot, like there was something in his eye.

"Yes, sir."

"I'm here to give you an orientation to Briarwood School, Oswald. The school's philosophy is based on the research of our founder, Dr. Kinnear. You are already acquainted with the thirty-seven rules. But basically it comes down to this: everybody in this school has come here because of discipline problems. We are here to educate you, but above all we are here to help you develop skills for better socialization." Mr. Akempis spoke in a singsongy monotone, like this was a canned speech he gave all the time.

"We have a merit/demerit system. If you do as you are instructed, you will remain in good standing. If you accumulate demerits, you will lose privileges. Sometimes demerits are referred to as 'DRs' or 'DR points.'" He waggled his fingers in the air, making little quotation marks. "All demerits are based on disrespect. Disrespect can come in many forms. Talking back, asking questions, making demands, these are all disrespectful. Fighting, littering, possession of weapons or drugs, grooming errors, and so on are all forms of disrespect. You will be expected to keep your hair above your ears and off your collar. You will be expected to wear the school uniform— jeans and a white T-shirt. In winter a jacket is optional. You will be expected to keep your clothes clean. Respect for yourself begins with good grooming."

Grooming errors? Boy, that really sucks, huh, Dad?

"You will live in the dormitory across the quadrangle. Reveille is at 5:55. PT—that's Physical Training—is at 6:00. Breakfast is at 7:20. Class begins at 8:20. Lunch is at 11:45. Classes end at 3:25. There are various group activities in the afternoon. Dinner is at 6:15. Study period is from 7:00 to 9:20. Then it's lights-out. You are expected to be prompt for all activities and classes. Tardiness will result in DRs. Failure to attend mandatory activities will result in DRs.

"Disrespect is something we watch for at all times. Talking back is obviously disrespectful. But disrespect can be conveyed in many ways. Rolling your eyes, sighing loudly, wisecracks— these are all forms of disrespect. We have zero tolerance for disrespect."

He smiled. His smile seemed as canned as his speech.

"Do you have any questions?"

"When can I talk to my mom?"

"Did I hear a 'sir' in there?"

"When can I talk to my mom, sir?"

"Your initial three months are probationary. Zero contact with parents. If you don't accumulate more than twenty DRs, you'll be eligible to call your parents once a week for ten minutes. After six months of good behavior, parents may come to visit."

Three months before I could even *talk* to my mother! I couldn't believe it. My heart sank. This was like going to prison. Maybe even worse! I bet even whacked-out serial killers on death row got to call their mothers every now and then.

"See the thing is, I really need to talk to my mom. I'm not even supposed to be here. My mom's new husband is this crazy guy who's trying to get me out of his life, so—"

Mr. Akempis held up his hand, waved it at me like he was

flagging down a taxi. "Mmp! Hup! Nope! Oswald, that's not our concern. You're here. Stick to the thirty-seven rules and you'll be fine. We're not interested in quote-unquote 'situations' here." He waggled his fingers in the air again.

I felt myself sliding and sliding and sliding down into the darkness. I was wasting my time trying to have a conversation with this guy.

I tried to think if I had any more questions, but nothing came to me. Rule One wasn't just a rule, it was a way of thinking. *Do not ask questions.* They meant it. You asked a question, you wouldn't like the answer.

"Good," Mr. Akempis said. "I'll take you over to the dormitory."

I stood up and walked to the door.

"Oh, by the way, your escape attempt? That's ten demerits. Therefore you now have ten demerits left to maintain good behavior standing."

"But . . . I didn't even know about the demerit thing when I ran away!" I said.

Mr. Akempis smiled his canned smile. "That's one demerit for back talk, Oswald. And one for not saying 'sir.'"

I stared at him.

The dean of students' little smile didn't waver. "Keep staring at me like that and you'll be down to seven points."

"Yes, sir," I said.

"That's more like it! I think you're going to do well here."

"Thank you, sir." I felt like such a phony suck-up loser. It was easy to see how the program worked here. The only way to get ahead was to act like a brainless robot. I'd always been a good kid. I even won the Good Citizen Award in middle school in eighth grade, me and Annabeth Porter. But even being the Good Citizen Award–type that I was, I wasn't sure I could pull off being a robot 24-7 for the next three months.

It made me really scared. What if I couldn't do it?

I turned and left the room.

So I'm writing this during study time in the dormitory. We have a room about the size of my bedroom at home, but it has six boys in it, including me. There's one desk. So if you want to write, you have to put your book on your lap. It doesn't seem like the way you'd design things if you actually wanted people to learn anything.

These are the guys in my room:

There's Sean Grainger—the kid who brought me the Pop-Tart. Turns out he's the fat boy who I saw crying because he couldn't keep up with the rest of the runners when I came in the first day. Everybody makes fun of him, but he seems really nice. Then there's a kind of irritating kid named Randall Cummings, Jr. He's always talking about how big his house is and how rich his dad is and how he has his own car even though he's not old enough to drive and stuff. Then there's this guy named Farhad Karroubi who cracks jokes all the time. The fourth guy is this tall black kid named Emmit Ellers. He seems pretty nice.

The last kid is older than us—or at least a lot bigger. His name's Mike Shepherd. Mike makes me nervous. He has a bunch of tattoos on his arms and hasn't said a word since I got here. He acts like we're not even here, just listening to music on his iPod and staring at the wall. Sean says he did something really bad to end up here, but he wouldn't tell me what it was. It's obvious everybody's afraid of Mike, though.

At nine twenty the lights went out. No warning, no nothing. Just click, and we were sitting there in total darkness. Somebody farted—I couldn't tell who—and everybody laughed.

It took me a long time to go to sleep. But finally I did.

Sometime in the night, though, something woke me up. I wasn't sure what it was at first, but then I saw. There was somebody standing over my bed. It was totally dark and I couldn't make out their face. My heart started beating really hard.

"What's happening?" I said.

The person standing above me put their hand over my mouth. I tried to wriggle out, but they were really strong.

Their face got close to mine and then a flashlight came on and I could see it was a man.

"Wrong one," a voice said. Not the guy standing over me, but somebody behind him, a woman.

The man let go of my mouth.

"There," the woman's voice said. "Him." I was pretty sure it was Mrs. Kinnear.

The guy standing over me moved to Sean's bed, grabbed Sean, and pulled him out of the bed. Sean's a pretty hefty kid, so the man must have been pretty strong. "What the—!" Sean said.

Then somebody yanked him to his feet. There was some rustling and bumping, like Sean was struggling.

"Hey!" I said. "What are you doing?"

Another voice, a kid's voice, coming from one of the bunks above me said, "Shut the hell up, Oz." It wasn't like he was mad. It was urgent, quiet—almost a whisper.

"You really shouldn't have given the new boy a Pop-Tart, Sean," the woman said. Her voice was soft and calm—but in a menacing way. I felt sick. Was he about to be punished in some horrible way just because of me?

"No!" Sean screamed. "Please! No!"

Then the door opened and he was gone. I could hear Sean screaming and crying all the way down the hallway.

"Where are they taking him?" I said after it got quiet. "What's going on here?"

One voice mumbled something that I couldn't quite make out.

"Silent broom?" I said. "Or did you say silent *room*?"

Another voice—I wasn't sure who it was, but it almost had to be Mike, the scary kid—said, "Nothing happened. Go back to sleep."

And after that nobody said anything.

I felt like I didn't sleep all night. But the next morning when the bugle blew for reveille, Sean was lying in his bunk, snoring away. I felt confused. Had I dreamed it? Had I dozed off while Sean came back?

I grabbed his shoulder and wiggled him until he woke up. He was staring at me with this dumb expression on his face.

"Are you okay?" I said.

"Huh?" he said.

"What happened last night?"

He stared at me for a minute like I was crazy, and for a

minute I thought maybe it was just a dream. But then suddenly he got this kind of hard look in his eye, like a curtain coming down, and he said, "I don't know what you're talking about." Then he rolled over, turning away from me.

"I'm sorry if you got in trouble about the Pop-Tart," I said. "I swear I didn't say anything to them about—"

"Shut up!" he said. "Just shut up!" And then he didn't move.

After that we went outside to do what they called PT—physical training. We had to run a mile and do jumping jacks and push-ups and that kind of thing. The drill-sergeant-looking guy who led PT was named Coach Bell. He was the gym teacher for Briarwood—and I think the guy who'd dragged Sean out of bed the night before. He shouted at everybody, calling us babies and girls and ladies and all that kind of stuff, but the exercise wasn't really that hard. Coach Bell called roll before the exercise. One of the kids wasn't there and he made a stink about it, saying he was going to give him two DRs. But for some reason he didn't call Sean's name, or make a big deal about the fact that he wasn't there.

After exercising, we went back to the dorm for showers. I ended up in the bathroom alone with Mike. He was brushing his teeth.

"What happened last night?" I said.

He didn't answer, didn't even look at me.

For a minute I thought maybe I should just shut up. But I had to know. "What did they do to Sean last night? Who was that in our room? Was it Coach Bell?"

Mike just stood there brushing his teeth like I wasn't even

there. Then suddenly, without any warning, he whirled around and slammed me up against the toilet stall, his tattooed forearm against my throat.

For a minute it was completely silent in the bathroom. His black eyes were staring right into mine. There was a dab of toothpaste on his chin. I thought maybe he was going to kill me. But then he put his face right up to my ear. "Don't sign anything," he whispered. It had definitely been his voice last night telling me to shut up.

"Huh?" Don't sign anything. What did that mean?

"Never, never, never, ever sign anything."

"What do you mean?"

He squeezed his arm tighter against my windpipe. Then suddenly he let go, went back to the sink and spit out his toothpaste.

I just stood there. After he finished rinsing his mouth out, he turned toward me like I'd just crapped on his foot. "What are *you* looking at, douche bag?"

"Hey," I said. "Whatever."

I held my hands up, then walked out.

Love,

Oz

twelve

Dear Dad,

After PT and showers we had the same crappy breakfast that I'd been eating all week, and then we went to class. There are about sixty kids at the school, and only three teachers. One was Mr. Akempis, the "dean of students" and one was a tired-looking lady named Miss Tulipwood, who sniffed a lot, and the third was a young guy named Mr. Wyman who needed a haircut, and went outside to smoke between every class. His fingers had a tiny tremor, like he was nervous. Only, he didn't seem nervous at all. Just bored. All three of the teachers just read out of the textbooks, droning on and on and on while kids slept or read books or drew pictures or cut up.

It seemed pretty much like a total joke schoolwise.

At lunch, Sean was already in the cafeteria when I came in with my tray of food. They served us greasy fried chicken, cold green beans, and a biscuit with sweet tea. I sat down at the table across from Sean. He started laughing and joking around like everything was totally normal.

The rest of the guys from my room all sat down with us—all except for Mike, who sat at a table by himself, glaring at his food. There weren't a lot of seats and I noticed this one kid who came into the cafeteria last ate standing up rather than sit with Mike.

"What's his story?" I said, pointing my fork at Mike.

Emmit Ellers was a tall, thin kid with short dreadlocks. "You don't want to mess with that dude," Emmit said.

"Why not?"

"Trust me," Sean said. "You just don't."

"I heard about this one kid," Farhad Karroubi said, raising one eyebrow comically, "who said something he didn't like? And Mike stuffed this kid in a trash can and then duct-taped the top on and rolled him down the hill into the swamp."

"Yeah," Randall Cummings said. "I heard that dude would have drowned if Mr. Wyman hadn't happened to walk by."

"Mr. Wyman seems nice enough," I said.

"Let me clue you in, dude," Sean said, suddenly losing his jokey expression. "There aren't any nice guys here. There're two kinds of people here—losers who do what they're told, and evil people."

Everybody at the table nodded.

"The teachers—Mr. Wyman, Miss Tulipwood, Mr. Akempis—they're losers," said Farhad.

"Mr. Pardee, Coach Bell," Emmit added. "They're evil."

"And Mrs. Kinnear, obviously," Farhad added.

Everybody nodded. "Totally evil."

"Dr. Kinnear is supposedly like a total saint," Farhad said. "But he's been really sick for a couple years. So he can't really do anything anymore. That's why the school sucks so much."

"He's in a wheelchair," Emmit said.

"If he only were better . . ." Farhad said.

". . . everything would be different," Sean said.

Nods all around and then a respectful silence.

"So Mrs. Kinnear actually runs the show around here," Emmit added.

Farhad laughed. "Dude, you ought to see all the teachers and staff around her. They're bowing and scraping and kissing butt like you wouldn't believe. They're petrified of her."

"With good reason," Randall Cummings said. Randall had a high, irritating voice. "She's—"

"Hey, can we talk about something else," Sean said.

Randall ignored him. "She's really evil. I mean the stuff she does to people—"

"Give it a rest!" Sean said.

"One time I got 'volunteered' to clean up their house and then she—"

"I said *shut up*," Sean said.

Randall looked at Sean. "You know you love it when she—"

Sean dove across the table and knocked Randall backward.

Before anything else could happen, Coach Bell had appeared. He grabbed Randall and hoisted him into the air by the shirt with one hand, then grabbed Sean's shirt and yanked the fat kid across the room and out the door.

The room was utterly silent for about ten seconds. "Uh-oh," Farhad said. "Somebody's racing the dog now."

Everybody laughed.

"What was that all about?" I said. "Why did Sean get so upset about Mrs. Kinnear?"

Everybody went silent, stopped laughing. "You'll find out soon enough," Farhad said drily.

That afternoon Randall and Sean weren't in class. After school was over I saw them running. They both looked completely exhausted, their shoes covered with mud, their shirts soaked with sweat. Behind them trotted two of the Dobermans.

"What's going on with them?" I said.

"When you do a real serious DR, sometimes they set the dogs on you," Emmit said. "You have to run and the dogs just follow after you. If you stop running, or you try to get off the path, the dogs will be on you like white on rice. They run you through the swamp and stuff."

In front of us, Sean stopped, dry heaved a couple times. The dogs came up behind him, started growling and barking. He started running again. His eyes were glazed. He ran right by us and didn't even seem to see us. He had briar scratches on his arms and legs, and his skin was covered with mosquito bites.

"Poor guy," I said.

"If he'd ever passed up a doughnut in his life," Emmit said, "it wouldn't be quite so hard on him."

That evening after dinner we were summoned to what was called "the auditorium"—which was really just a big room with cheap linoleum floors. We sat around for a while in silence, with Coach Bell glaring at us. In the front of the room was a large easel with red velvet draped over it. You could make out the outlines of some kind of big poster or picture underneath the velvet. Then finally the door opened and Mrs. Kinnear entered, looking very dramatic with her pale skin and glossy black hair. She was expensively dressed, like she was a lawyer going into court or something.

She walked to the front of the room and said, "Good evening, scholars."

"Good evening, Mrs. Kinnear," everyone said.

Mrs. Kinnear looked around the room. She seemed to be searching for something to complain about. But then, suddenly, she smiled. Her teeth were perfect and very white, straight out of a toothpaste commercial.

"I have marvelous news, scholars," she said. "The Briarwood School has recently been the recipient of a generous donation from our chairman of the board, Mr. Martin Shugrue, which will allow us to dramatically expand our physical plant. Mr. Akempis, if you would be so kind?"

The wormy little "dean of students," Mr. Akempis, dragged the easel closer to Mrs. Kinnear. He handed her the tasseled end of a gold cord attached to the velvet drape. Mrs. Kinnear yanked the cord and the easel wobbled a little bit, almost falling over. Mr. Akempis grabbed it, righted it, and the velvet fell away from a large architectural drawing.

"Scholars, let me present to you the Martin R. Shugrue Student Activity Center!"

Everybody sat there like lumps. I guess everybody felt pretty confident it would be another crappy building like all the rest of the buildings on campus.

"Scholars," Mrs. Kinnear said, "as you know, Parents Day is coming up next Sunday. Those of you who have been here for at least six months, and who have not accumulated more than twenty DRs, will be permitted to see your parents for an hour in the afternoon and then to attend the formal banquet that evening. Today you are seeing a preview of the new activity center that will be the culmination of Dr. Kinnear's dreams for this school. On the morning of Parents Day, bulldozers will begin clearing all the brush behind our home all the way down to the edge of the lake. At the culmination of the banquet, we'll officially break ground."

The room was silent for a moment. Then someone whispered loudly, "Oh *great*." I couldn't be sure, but I thought it was Emmit. I wondered why he cared.

Mrs. Kinnear whirled around, glared at the room.

"Who said that?" Her voice wasn't loud, but there was something incredibly frightening about it.

No one spoke.

She continued to survey the room with her cold green eyes. Then, suddenly, it was like somebody threw a switch and her big toothpaste smile came on again. "Well! Come on then. Let's have a big Briarwood cheer for our new plan."

Everybody cheered. But not like they really meant it. Mrs. Kinnear surveyed the room like she was waiting to see who stopped cheering first so she could punish them somehow. Finally the apathetic cheering wound down.

"In the meantime," she continued, "there is a great deal of work to be done to make the campus presentable for your parents. All normal activities, sports practices, and so on will be suspended for the week. Dean Akempis will be organizing work crews. There's painting, cleaning, woodwork, and a great deal more to be done."

The room was silent. You could tell everybody was thinking, *This sucks.* But nobody said it, of course.

"Dr. Kinnear wishes to offer his apologies for not appearing here personally to convey the wonderful news about the new campus activity center," she said. "But he asked me to pass on one thing to you. As you know, he believes that you are all good boys. So today, he's extending to each and every one of you a one-time offer. If all of you will demonstrate exemplary behavior for the next week, he will allow all of you to meet your parents—even those of you who have accumulated more than twenty DRs."

There was another cheer. This time everybody sounded like they meant it. I joined in, too. *I'd get to see Mom!* That meant I'd have a chance to explain the dirty tricks that Don had played on me. And maybe she'd take me away from here.

Mrs. Kinnear held up her hands and the room gradually got quiet.

"Naturally," she said, "this applies only to those of you who are past the three-month probation period."

I groaned, feeling my hopes slip away. It was like getting kicked in the stomach.

Mrs. Kinnear talked some more, but I didn't really listen. When she finally stopped talking, everybody cheered in this fake way and she left the room.

As we were filing out, Emmit said, "We are so hosed."

"How are we going to get it done?" Farhad said.

Just then Mike walked up behind them and said, "Hey, shut up! The new kid's standing right next to you."

"Sorry, Mike!" Farhad said.

Mike shoved Farhad so he banged into Emmit. "Are you out of your minds?" Mike said to them. Then he stalked away.

"What's he got his panties in a wad about?" I said.

Emmit and Farhad shook their heads sharply, looked away. "Uh, nothing," Farhad said. "It was nothing, dude."

This place is very confusing, Dad. It's like everybody's hiding something. I'm starting to feel like this whole place is one big nasty secret.

Your son,

Oz

thirteen

Dear Dad,

Well, it was another weird night.

I went to bed and fell straight to sleep. But at some point I woke up. I heard people moving around in the room. I was thinking, *Oh, no, here we go again.* Only, after a second, I realized it was just the guys in the room who were moving around.

Somebody bumped into something and kind of laughed and then somebody else told him to be quiet. Then the window opened and somebody threw something out. My eyes started adjusting to the dark and I saw that Emmit was standing there with a rope in his hand that had been made out of bedsheets.

"Dude!" he whispered. "Hurry."

Then he climbed out the window.

I should point out here that the front door of the dorm is locked every night and only Coach Bell has the key. Plus there's a night watchman who sits at a little booth outside the door to make sure nobody leaves.

I lay there without moving, watching as all the other kids in the room—including Mike—climbed slowly out the window. After a minute the rope came sailing back in the window. Somebody had attached a rock to the end of it and thrown it back inside so that nobody would see it dangling there against the wall.

I waited a second, then got up and looked out the window. I could see the kids sneaking across the quadrangle toward the woods that were between us and the lake. In fact, they were walking toward the exact area where Mrs. Kinnear had said the new student activity building was going to be built.

I pulled on my jeans and shoes and tossed the rope back out the window. The rope made a soft thump against the wall. I climbed down, threw the rope back inside the room, then headed across the quadrangle. It was spooky dark. When you grow up near a city, you're used to all this light in the sky that's thrown up by the lights in the city. But here, there was nothing. No city lights, no street lamps, nothing but stars. There wasn't even a moon.

By the time I got down to the ground, the guys from my room had disappeared into the woods on the far end of the quad. I wished I had thought to bring a flashlight. But now it was too late. It suddenly occurred to me to wonder how we would get back in. But I figured my roommates had thought about that.

I walked quickly across the weedy ground to the scrubby forest. Once I got there, I realized I had no idea where my roommates had gone. I looked back to see if anybody was watching me. Nothing moved. Then I noticed a light. At the very top of the headmaster's house was a single window. It must have been in the attic on the third floor. Silhouetted in the window was the figure of a man. I couldn't make out his face. Was it Dr. Kinnear? Was he watching me? I couldn't tell. Suddenly the light winked off and he was gone.

My heart was pounding. I decided I'd better get into the woods—even if I didn't know where I was going. It was better than getting spotted.

I walked slowly into the woods. It was a scrubby pine forest, very different from the planted pines I'd run into when I'd tried to escape the first day. This was just barely more than a thicket, the pine trees all small and thin and packed together so that it was hard going to make any progress through them. Branches hit me in the face and brambles scratched my legs. I started thinking, *This is really stupid.*

The farther I went, the darker it got. I realized I had no idea where I was going. None whatsoever. Somewhere an owl hooted—at least I hoped it was an owl—a loud eerie screech. I heard something moving in the woods near me—a scrabbling, rasping sound that I was pretty sure wasn't a kid. A rat? A snake? Mosquitoes whined in the air around me. They were biting me on the face, the neck, the arms, even on my ankles in the space between my shoes and the bottom of my jeans.

I looked back. Or . . . what I thought was back. Only I couldn't see anything behind me. No lights, no buildings, no nothing. I could have been going in circles for all I knew. I turned around, started going back. But after five minutes of bumbling around, I was still in the middle of the dark woods.

I was totally lost. I wanted to start running. But I figured that wouldn't do me any good either. I just felt alone and scared.

Just as I felt like I was about to freak out and start crying like a little kid, suddenly I broke out of the woods and found myself on the edge of the lake. A thin sliver of moon had just begun to peek over the horizon, leaving a broken silver trail on the oily black surface of the water.

Okay, I figured. If I just walked along the edge of the water, I'd eventually run into the boat landing. From there I'd take the trail that led back to the campus.

I began moving quickly down the shoreline, splashing through pools of slimy water. It was slow going. There were logs and cypress knees and all kinds of junk in the swampy land next to the lake. And then I saw the boat landing coming up. I took a deep breath. I never thought I would have been happy to see the Briarwood School again. But suddenly the idea of seeing the crappy old dormitory again seemed pretty welcoming.

Between me and the landing was a small pond, not more than thirty feet across. If it was like the ones I'd been in before, it was probably only a few inches deep.

Only, as I found out when I began walking into it—it wasn't like the others. I slipped, felt something give way underneath me. And suddenly I was up to my waist in slimy water.

Remember those nature shows you and me used to watch on Discovery Channel, Dad? As soon as I fell into that water, I started thinking about all those shows about alligators. I could hear the voice of the cheesy narrator in my head:

The alligator rarely attacks humans. But unusually large alligators have been known to treat people as prey. In one particularly grisly example . . .

Then I thought, *Hey, come on. It's just thirty feet. Swim it.* I was a good swimmer. There was nothing to it. All I had to do was get to that big log on the other side of the little pond and haul myself up. And I'd be home free.

Which is when the huge log on the other side of the pond winked and slid slowly off the bank into the pond, barely making a ripple in the algae-covered water.

My heart about exploded. That was no log. It was a gator!

When I finally stopped running, I was way down the bank of the lake. I mean, *way* down. No telling how far I had run.

I stopped, sat down on a cypress knee, and tried to catch my breath. *Okay,* I thought. Worst-case scenario, I'd sit there by the lake till the sun came up. When it started getting light, I'd be able to find my way back. And maybe I'd be able to sneak back in with the other kids when they came out and lined up for morning exercise with Coach Bell.

I don't know how long I sat there, but it seemed like forever. I just watched the lake. It was kind of beautiful actually. I mean, if you weren't more or less marooned there at the worst time of your whole life, it would have been pretty cool.

Then I noticed something gleaming. Not glowing, but gleaming—like metal reflecting light. What was it? I couldn't tell. The night was too dark. I sat for a while, listening to the mosquitoes swarming around my head. I was about to go crazy itching. At this rate I was going to be drained of blood by the time the sun came up.

Finally I decided that I'd go see what the gleam was coming from. It was boring just sitting there. Plus I figured a moving target would be just slightly harder for the mosquitoes to eat. I walked slowly toward the gleam. Definitely metal. Maybe aluminum?

It took about five minutes, but finally I got there. And when I did, I began to make sense of what I was seeing. It was a boat—an airboat like the one I'd come to the school on with Mr. Edson. Only this one looked like it was about a million years old—the paint chipped off, vines growing through it, the pontoons sunk down in the mud.

I was staring at it when suddenly I heard something, a crack of a twig behind me. I whirled around to see who it was.

But it was too late. Somebody grabbed me and threw me to the ground. I felt my head bang into the ground and everything went kind of gray and fuzzy for a second.

By the time I recovered my senses, somebody was on top of me and there was something sharp poking into my throat.

"Don't move!" a voice whispered.

Then a light came on in my face.

There was a brief silence.

"Oh hell!" a voice said. The person who was straddling my chest. It was Emmit.

Suddenly all around me I heard laughter, four or five kids laughing like crazy. It was my roommates.

"It's Oz," Sean said.

"Oh, man!" I said. "Y'all scared the poop out of me."

"You scared *us*, dude," Farhad said.

Then suddenly nobody was laughing. I looked up and there was Mike scowling over us.

"Somebody's gonna hear us, you idiots," Mike said quietly. But not quiet enough to take the menace out of his voice.

There was a long silence. Finally Mike said, "We gotta get rid of him."

"Get *rid* of him?" Sean said. "What's that mean?"

More silence.

"We don't know anything about this kid," Mike said.

"Yeah," Sean said. "But . . ."

"But what? He could be a plant. He could be working for *them*."

I didn't have to think hard to figure out who he meant by "them."

"We gotta get rid of him," Mike said.

Emmit said, "Dude, are you saying what I think you're saying? Like . . . *killing* him?"

Mike just looked at Emmit.

"Hey, forget it," Emmit said.

"Yeah," Farhad said. "I mean, come on."

Mike looked at the other kids, then shook his head disgustedly. "You people make me sick," he said. "You're like a bunch of four-year-old girls."

"Dude—"

"Don't *dude* me," Mike said. "You know what this place is." He waved vaguely in the direction of the campus. "It's us or them."

"Yeah, but . . ."

Mike turned around and walked away. "To hell with y'all," he said. Then he looked at his watch. "Anyway, it's time to get back." He stalked away, disappearing into the darkness.

We just stood there until we couldn't hear him anymore.

Finally Emmit got up and dusted himself off, then pulled me up, too. "I don't think he meant it," he said.

"Yeah," Sean said. "I think he's just trying to scare you."

"What's going on here?" I said.

My roommates looked at one another like they were trying to figure out what to tell me.

Finally Sean leaned toward me and, with a mysterious smile, whispered, "We have a plan. . . ."

When we got back to the dormitory, Mike was standing under the window, staring up at our room.

"Where's the string?" Emmit said, turning toward me.

"Huh?" I said.

"The string, dude! There was a string tied to the end of the rope. That way we could grab the string and pull the rope back out the window."

"Uh . . ." I said.

"You dumbass," Mike said in a voice of disgust. "Now we're screwed."

"I hope you're proud of yourself, *Oswald*," Randall said.

"Aw, leave him alone," Emmit said. "He didn't know."

"His ignorance is not gonna help us get back in," Randall said.

"I told you," Mike said, shaking his head.

"What do we do?" Sean said, his lip suddenly quivering a little.

"We'll hide behind the maintenance shed and wait till PT," Mike said. "Hopefully we can come out one at a time before lineup, and Coach Bell won't notice."

"What about my clothes?" I said. "I fell in the swamp and I've got algae and crap all over me."

Mike looked at me for a long time, his black eyes boring into me. "I don't really give a damn what happens to you," he said. Then he moved closer, put his finger in my chest and pushed me lightly. "But if you rat us out, son, I'm not joking, your little ass is dead."

We waited behind the shed until the horn blew for PT and kids started straggling out the door of the dorm. "You're last," Mike said to me.

My roommates waited until Coach Bell's back was turned and then filtered slowly out into the crowd. After they had all gone, I slipped out, too.

"Line up, ladies!" Coach Bell screamed.

We lined up, and he called roll. As he was doing the roll call, Mrs. Kinnear appeared wearing a very tight red jogging suit, her black hair up in a ponytail. I don't know how old she was—maybe in her late thirties—but she had a body most girls my age would have killed for. She walked slowly by us, scanning the lines of kids, until finally her cold green eyes stopped on me.

"Excuse me, Coach Bell," she said, "but may I interrupt?"

"Of course, ma'am."

"You remember what I said," a voice whispered, so quietly that I could barely hear it. It was Mike, standing in line just behind me. I felt something sharp poke against my ribs. It felt like the point of a knife.

Mrs. Kinnear approached me and the knife point in my back went away.

"Oswald?" she said. "And how are we today?"

"Fine, ma'am." My heart was going *gzzzh gzzzh gzzzh*.

A cold smile formed on Mrs. Kinnear's face. "Oz," she said, "what's the third rule?"

"Respect for yourself is respect for others, ma'am," I said.

"Rule Fourteen?"

"Good grooming is the foundation of self-respect. Ma'am."

"Mm." She kept smiling, then she reached out with a red-nailed finger and plucked the sleeve of my disgusting-looking T-shirt. "And do you consider yourself to be well-groomed at this moment, Oswald?"

"I, ah, slipped in a puddle coming out to PT."

"That wasn't what I asked. Do you consider yourself, at this very moment, to be well-groomed?"

"Uh. No, definitely not, ma'am."

She looked around the quadrangle, blinking curiously. "A puddle? Oswald, it hasn't rained in almost ten days."

I didn't say anything. I just stared straight ahead like a soldier.

"Rule Twenty-one?"

"Lying is an offense against yourself and others, ma'am."

"Lying is an offense against yourself and others. Don't you agree?"

"Yes, ma'am."

"Young man, you don't even know me. Why would you lie to me in such a blatantly offensive and insulting way? Did you *mean* to hurt my feelings?" Her smile got even bigger, showing off her beautiful teeth. "Or are you just stupid?"

I kept standing there. I wanted to punch her in the face.

"Seriously," she said, "I'd like an answer. Mean? Stupid? Stupid, mean? It really has to be one or the other."

"Uh . . . stupid, ma'am?"

A couple of kids snickered.

Mrs. Kinnear's head snapped around and they shut up quick.

"Oswald," she said. "I think you just tried to escape again. Tell me how you did it."

I didn't say anything.

"Now," she said. Her voice was hard as a diamond.

"I . . . jumped out the window. Then I went in the woods and fell in a pond."

"There's just no place to escape to, is there?"

"No, ma'am."

She kept smiling at me. "Well, I guess the bad news for you is that's eight DR points for you. You're down to zero now. So you can pretty much forget about seeing Mommy and Daddy for the next six months." Then she cocked her head. "Oh, I forgot. There's no Daddy, is there? How tragic."

I felt like telling her not to talk about you, Dad. But I was too scared. So I just stood there like a stone.

"Coach Bell?" Mrs. Kinnear called. "Would you tell Dean Akempis that Oz has been relieved of his academic responsibilities for the day? I've got just a *ton* of things to do in preparation for Parents Day. Oz is going to be my little personal assistant for the day."

Somebody laughed nervously.

"Yes, ma'am," Coach Bell said.

"Go inside, Oswald," Mrs. Kinnear said. "Take a hot shower,

put on some clean clothes, and then report to the headmaster's house."

"Yes, ma'am."

Everybody stood in line, staring at me while I walked back toward the dorm. There was no snickering. If anything, they all looked kind of scared.

"Don't piss her off," some kid whispered as I walked by. "You don't want to end up in the Silent Room."

The Silent Room. That was the second time somebody had mentioned the Silent Room thing. What were they talking about?

Dad, I get more scared all the time. I keep thinking things will get better. But they just get worse and worse. And worse.

Love,

Oz

fourteen

Dear Dad,

Well, I didn't like Mrs. Kinnear much the first time I met her—but now I pretty much hate her. She worked me like a slave today. But even so, something good happened.

I showed up at the headmaster's house and Mrs. Kinnear met me at the door. The first thing she did was make me take my shoes off. She was worried about tracking dirt onto the white carpet. I'd expected the old house to have lots of antiques and gloomy furniture and stuff, but actually it was real modern-looking inside, with glass-topped tables and modern art on the walls. Then she made me put on surgical gloves and start cleaning her house. Surgical gloves!

First came the bathrooms. Before I got started, she handed me this little laminated card that had a list of instructions. She made me read it out loud. It had all her specifications for how the toilet was to be cleaned, how the shower was to be cleaned, what kind of soap, what kind of disinfectant, all this type of stuff.

I got started, cleaning like mad. After a while she came to see what I'd done, and then she yelled at me for cleaning the glass door the wrong way. "No abrasive cleansers on the glass door!" she screamed. "What are you, an imbecile? It says right here, instruction number nine! No abrasive cleansers on the—"

"Yes, ma'am." I couldn't tell you what an abrasive cleanser was. But apparently using it on glass was a very big deal.

After that was over, she made me go upstairs and vacuum the floors. She had a specific pattern for how you vacuumed, too, and there was more screaming when I went back and forth where I was supposed to have gone up and down or something. Then she left me alone for a while with more directions and more chores.

While I was working, this girl came out of a room and looked at me. I assumed she must be Mrs. Kinnear's daughter. She had the same jet-black hair, though her face didn't look like Mrs. Kinnear's at all. She was about my age, very pretty, but not in a scary, dramatic way like her mom. She was wearing fuzzy pink pajamas and had her black hair twisted up on her head in a kind of messy way, held in place with chopsticks.

"Lucky you," she said, after watching me for a minute. She had a playful glint in her eyes.

"Yes, ma'am," I said.

"Jesus Christ," she said, laughing, "they really got you brainwashed, huh? You don't have to call me ma'am."

"What should I call you?"

"I'm Camryn," she said. "Who are you?"

"Oz."

"Oz?" She raised one eyebrow. "That's kinda cool."

"I better get back to work," I said. "Or your mom's gonna kill me."

"*Step*mom," she said. "Totally psycho-bitch stepmom."

I tried to look noncommittal.

"Dr. Kinnear's my dad," she said. "He married Gwen about two years ago and my life has been complete hell ever since."

"I know *that* story," I said.

"Your dad married a psycho bitch, too?"

"Other way around. My mom married a psycho jerk. That's how I ended up here."

"Bummer."

I nodded. "So do you live here all year round?" I said. "Where do you go to school?"

"Nah, I go to boarding school. *Did* anyway. I got thrown out last week for . . ." She shrugged. ". . . you know—some stuff. So Dad and Psycho Bitch are trying to figure out what to do with me next."

"I would think it would kinda suck to be the only girl on the whole island."

"You have no idea. It's *so* boring here. I feel like shooting myself every day I'm here." Then she gave me this flirty little smile. "But it has its advantages." She waved at me with the tips of her fingers and disappeared back into her room.

I started vacuuming again.

Basically I spent the rest of the day getting screamed at by Mrs. Kinnear. Every now and then I'd see Camryn walking by in some other room and she'd meet my eye and then glance at her stepmom and roll her eyes or make a face or something, and I'd have to concentrate really hard so I didn't laugh.

Mrs. Kinnear didn't make lunch for me or offer me anything to drink or let me go to the cafeteria. I just kept working like a slave. Finally, around three o'clock, she went over to the administration building to do something and Camryn came down from her room. I had just vacuumed the living room and now I was dusting. Camryn had her hair down now. It was about shoulder length and she was wearing a baggy T-shirt with the name of some old heavy metal band on it, cutoff cargo pants, and bare feet. Very nice legs, too, let me say.

"Psycho Bitch didn't make you any lunch, did she?" she said.

I shook my head.

"You want a sandwich or something?"

"I probably better not," I said.

"Hey, don't worry about it," she said. Then she went away.

A few minutes later she came back with a sandwich on a plate, with a pickle and some barbecue potato chips.

"It's just baloney," she said, shrugging.

I wolfed it down. I hadn't had breakfast or lunch and after all my adventures during the night, I was starving. She watched me eat with this funny expression on her face.

When I was done eating, she said, "So how come you're here?"

"My stepdad framed me."

"No, seriously, what'd you do to get sent here? You must have done something bad. Smoke a little ganja? Flunk out of civics? Steal a car?"

"I'm being totally serious. I'm like this nice normal kid. I won the Good Citizen Award in eighth grade for godsake. I don't do drugs or beat up little kids or run away from home or steal TVs. My stepdad basically framed me so it looked like I was this bad kid. Then he convinced Mom to send me here. Like it's all for my own good."

She stared at me. "You're serious."

"Totally."

"Dude, that *sucks.*"

"No kidding."

We sort of hung out for a while and then I heard the front door open and Camryn gave me this comical look and picked up the plate I'd eaten from and went tiptoeing off to the kitchen in this really exaggerated way. I couldn't help smiling.

"What are you smirking about?" Mrs. Kinnear said, sweeping into the room.

"Nothing, ma'am," I said.

Mrs. Kinnear ran a finger across the top of a picture frame, stared suspiciously at her finger, obviously hoping to find a trace of dust. Unable to find fault there, she scanned the room. Then her eyes lit on something. I looked down. There on the carpet, about the size of a dime, was a small orange flake.

She bent over, lifted it triumphantly. "What," she said, "is *this?*"

It was obviously a piece of barbecue potato chip.

"This was *not* here when I left, Oswald." She waited for me to say something, but I just acted dumb. "This is a potato chip, Oswald. Have you been stealing food from my home?"

"No, ma'am."

She stared at me, then reached out with her long red fingernail and touched my cheek. When her finger came away, there was a tiny fleck of orange on her nail. She smiled at me. "Liar, liar, pants on fire," she said.

"Ma'am, I didn't steal anything."

"Then please explain."

I stood there with my mouth moving, but nothing came out.

"That's five DR points. You're now into negative territory." She clicked her fingernails on the door frame a few times. "Which means we're going to have to start exploring more aggressive forms of behavior modification."

"Uh, Mother?" It was Camryn, standing on the far end of the room. "I had a snack. It was my potato chips. I offered him a couple, that's all. He's not lying."

Mrs. Kinnear whirled around. "How many times have I told you, young lady, about eating food on the white carpet? Never. Eat. Food. On. The. White. Carpet."

Camryn nodded, looking real serious. "I forgot. I'm very sorry, Mother."

"Up to your room, young lady. Now!" She turned back to me, and Camryn stuck out her tongue then walked away with her fingers held out in the air, doing an imitation of the way Mrs. Kinnear walked. "You dodged that one, young man," she said. "But don't let it happen again."

"Let what happen, ma'am?"

Mrs. Kinnear's eyes narrowed. "She is a very naive and trusting girl. You will not speak to her. You will not accept food from her. I don't want you even *looking* at her. Clear?"

"Yes, ma'am."

Mrs. Kinnear kept me at it until after supper was over. Finally, around eight that night she said, "Alright. You're done for now."

As I was leaving the house something hit the ground near me. I bent over and picked it up. It was a shiny new key.

Where had it come from? I frowned at it, then looked up behind me. I could see somebody silhouetted in the window above. It was Camryn. She gave me a little wave, then held something up to the window. A piece of paper.

Written in pink Magic Marker was a message: I'M SOOOOO BORED!

I was afraid Mrs. Kinnear would see me, so I was kind of nervous and started to turn around. But Camryn held up another sign.

COME SEE ME.

Then another.

ANY TIME. The word *any* was underlined about five times.

She waved with just her fingertips, stuck out her tongue, and then disappeared. I tucked the key in my pocket. Even though I was starving to death and exhausted, I felt this little flood of happiness inside me.

Why did stuff like that never happen to me in school? At home, cute girls never even gave me a second look.

So, I don't know, Dad. I guess good things can happen even in the crappiest places.

Love,

Oz

fifteen

Dear Dad,

Everybody was in a gloomy mood when I got back to the room.

"It's worse than I thought," Mike was saying as I walked in.

I guess before I get into that though, I need to tell you about The Plan.

It started like this:

The other day when Sean was being chased around through the woods by the dogs, he lost his way and somehow got off the trail. The dogs started freaking out because he was going the wrong way, so he started thrashing around trying to get back on the trail and he was getting more and more lost, and the dogs were getting more and more crazy. And suddenly he saw this gleam over in the bushes by the lake. As he ran by it, he realized it was an old airboat. When he got back he told everybody about the boat.

Usually Mike doesn't talk to anybody. But this time, according to the way Sean told it to me, he had suddenly jumped off his bunk and said, "Hold up, Sean. Who else have you told?"

Sean had said, "Nobody."

"Keep it that way," Mike had said.

"Why?" Sean had said.

Mike had said, "How many ways off this island are there?"

"One?"

"Correct. The airboat. Which is kept in a locked boathouse with a motorized door. Mr. Pardee sleeps in the boathouse. Even if you got the key, you'd have to crank the motor to open the door and Mr. Pardee would hear you. So we're all pretty well stuck here."

"Okay . . ." Sean had said.

"This airboat you found—if we could get it started," Mike had said, "then we could get off the island, couldn't we? We could escape."

"Yeah, but none of us know anything about airboats."

Mike had said, "Just to piss my old man off I went to the vocational program at my high school. I took classes in auto mechanics. If y'all helped me out, I bet we could do it."

And so the great escape plan was hatched.

It was a great plan, except for one thing. The day after they found the airboat was the day Mrs. Kinnear announced the new building. On Parents Day—which was only a week away—a bunch of bulldozers would arrive to level the area. At which point Mrs. Kinnear would find out there was an airboat stuck in the mud by the lake. She was not stupid. She would immediately either have it destroyed or tow it into the boathouse and lock it up. Either way, if the great escape was to work, we'd have to get the airboat fixed in six days.

So anyway, when I had blundered into them, my roommates had just gone down there for the first time to clean up the boat and see what the likelihood was that they could get the airboat operating in just six days.

"You're talking about the boat?" I said as I sagged down onto the bed.

"Obviously," Mike said.

Sean said, "So did Mrs. Kinnear give you any food?"

I shook my head.

He rummaged around in his footlocker, came out with a cold hamburger and some greasy, limp fries. "Don't say I never did anything for you," he said.

I tore into the cold food, and it seemed like the best burger and fries I'd had in my life.

"The good news," Mike said, "is that the engine on the airboat is really old. I bet it's been sitting there for thirty years. It's a Ford small block from the sixties. Simple design. Simple parts. Not that much to go wrong."

"So what's the bad news?" Emmit said.

"The bad news is that the engine is really old."

Farhad chimed in, "I thought that was good news."

"My point is, it's all rusted and messed up. I'll have to take it totally apart, degrease everything, clean off the rust. Maybe— if we totally luck out—it'll start."

"Plus you need a battery," I said.

Mike looked at me sharply. "Plus we need a battery." He kept looking at me. "How did you know that?"

I kept chewing. Finally when I finished my hamburger, I said, "Common sense. Everybody knows you need a battery to start an engine. If it's been sitting there for years, of course it's dead."

"Can we do it?" Emmit said.

Mike clapped his hands. "Get in bed. Get some sleep. We're gonna be up every night for the next six days."

Of course, Dad, you know why I knew about the battery. Common sense? Yeah, maybe. But you know there's more to it than that.

You taught me a lot of stuff before you died. Probably more than you even knew. I'm thinking maybe for the first time in my life, it'll come in handy.

Love,

Oz

sixteen

Dear Dad,

I have to get off this island. I can just see that if I stay here, things won't go well. I think that airboat is my only hope. Can we fix up an engine in six days? With no spare parts and no tools? I doubt it. But we've got to try.

It seemed like I had just fallen asleep when I was awakened. Noise in the room.

I thought it was probably the other kids, ready to go work on the airboat. But then I felt a pair of hands clamping around my neck.

"Up!" a voice said.

Flashlight in the face.

"Up, now." It was Coach Bell, with somebody standing be-hind him.

The other kids were stirring around now. I could feel the fear in the room. This was the point at which Sean had started screaming the other night. Where were we going? What terrible thing was about to happen to me?

I barely had a chance to think before Coach Bell had me out the door and marching down the hallway. I knew better than to ask questions. I just kept my mouth shut and walked. I was still bleary and confused from sleep, but my heart was pounding and my hands were shaking. We marched across the quad and over to the administration building. Up the steps, through the door, up a dark paneled staircase, and into a very large room with an old banquet table in the middle.

Sitting at the far end of the table was a thin, pale man with black hair, graying at the temples. Behind him, turned away from me, was a second man, balding and short of chubby, just under normal height, wearing a blue suit and a bow tie. He didn't turn around when I entered.

The seated man lifted his hand slowly, pointed to the far end of the table. "Please, Oswald," he said. "Sit."

I sat at the chair on the other end of the very long table. The black-haired man began to move toward me. It was only then that I saw he was in a motorized wheelchair. He was very tired-looking, very thin, and one of his arms hung limply in his lap. But he had a kind smile on his face.

"I apologize for bringing you out at this hour, Oswald," he said. He had a rich, pleasant voice that seemed kind of strange coming out of his emaciated-looking body. "My name is Dr. Kinnear."

He drove the little wheelchair using a joystick with his left hand. When he came even with me, he held out his left hand and I shook it awkwardly. His grip felt soft and weak.

"As you probably know, Oswald," Dr. Kinnear said, "I'm the headmaster of the Briarwood School. I'm sorry I didn't have a chance to welcome you earlier, but my health is a little dodgy these days." He smiled a little sadly. "Anyway, if there's anything I can do for you, please let me know. Most of the day-to-day operations of the school are taken care of by my wife. But I want you to know that I care for each and every boy in this school. I want you to succeed and thrive. So please, don't hesitate."

"Thank you, sir," I said.

"Again, I also apologize for getting you out of bed. I understand you've had a very busy day. But there are a few administrative details regarding your stay with us that need to be handled." He gestured at the man in the suit, who was still occupied with reading something on the sideboard. "Martin Shugrue is the chairman of our board of directors. He's a very busy man and so we have to seize the moment whenever he has the opportunity to join us."

Mr. Shugrue turned toward us and smiled. He was a soft-faced man with a five o'clock shadow and a few strands of dark hair slicked way across his balding head. There was something about him that I instinctively didn't like. He reminded me of a sleazy lawyer on one of those legal shows on TV.

"Mr. Shugrue likes to meet each of our scholars personally, and handle a few of the administrative details himself," Dr. Kinnear said.

Mr. Shugrue walked over and shook my hand. Unlike Dr. Kinnear's, his grip was firm and businesslike. "Pleased to meet you, son," he said.

"If there's nothing else, Martin . . ." Dr. Kinnear said.

Mr. Shugrue shook his head.

"Well, I'm feeling a bit tired," Dr. Kinnear said to me. "So if you don't mind, I'll leave you in the capable hands of Mr. Shugrue."

"Yes, sir," I said.

Mr. Shugrue opened the door, and Dr. Kinnear drove out of the room in his wheelchair. After he was gone, Mr. Shugrue shut the door, walked over, and sat down. "I'm famished," he said. "I'm sure you've already eaten, but I know how growing boys are. You want to join me for a bite?"

"Oh, wow," I said. "Yes, sir, that would be great."

"Fabulous!" He clapped his hands together. Immediately the door opened and the old lady who ran the school cafeteria hobbled in pushing a little cart with dishes on it. She plunked one of them down in front of Mr. Shugrue, then one in front of me. The smell was incredible. There was a big steak, a potato, asparagus with some kind of fancy-looking yellow sauce on it. I couldn't believe that the same old lady who made all our crappy cafeteria food had made this.

"What's the wine, Mrs. Ellis?" The old lady pointed to a bottle on the cart. Mr. Shugrue picked it up, studied the label.

Mrs. Ellis went away and Mr. Shugrue poured the red liquid into a glass. "I know it's against policy," he said, "but here, have a taste." He poured about an inch of wine into the wineglass in front of me.

I looked at it nervously. "Uh. I don't drink."

"Hey, son, it's not vodka for Pete's sake." He winked at me, tasted the wine. "I was raised in France. Kids there have a little taste starting when they're eight or ten years old. They get used to it, see, and so there's no alcoholism problem. Very rational approach." He lifted his glass, sloshed it around, held it up to the light, then sniffed it, then held it up to the light again. Only after all this monkeying around did he finally taste it, swishing it around in his mouth. "Oh, that's nice! Try it. It's a '99 Château Margaux. Three hundred and ten bucks a bottle, worth every nickel."

"Yes, sir." Rule one, don't ask questions—right? I tasted the wine. It tasted okay, I guess, but I didn't see what the big deal was. I was a lot more interested in the steak. I sawed off a big piece and started chewing. Suddenly I was in heaven.

"So tell me about yourself, Oswald," Mr. Shugrue said.

I told him a few things between bites. As soon as there was a brief pause, Mr. Shugrue started talking again. I could see he was one of those guys who asked questions but then didn't really listen to you because he already had all the answers. He talked about the business he was in, and all the reasons he was so successful, and talked all kinds of junk that even a fifteen-year-old kid could tell were just dopey clichés.

I concentrated on eating. After a while my mouth got a little dry. There was nothing to drink but the wine, so that's what I drank. Soon I got used to it and it started tasting kind of good.

Mr. Shugrue talked and talked and I ate and ate, and he kept pouring wine every time I had a sip, so I couldn't really tell if I was drinking a lot or not. After a while, though, I started feeling good, and Mr. Shugrue started seeming like a nice guy and I started wondering why I'd felt so suspicious of him before.

When we were done eating, Mrs. Ellis brought in some cheesecake. "Flown in fresh from New York," Mr. Shugrue said. "You like it?"

"Mm!" I said. My mouth was full.

And then, finally, we were done.

Mr. Shugrue poured himself some more wine. But this time he didn't pour any for me.

"Well!" he said. "So I understand you got off to a little bit of a rocky start at Briarwood, huh?"

I shrugged.

He clapped me on my shoulder. "Hey, believe me, I know what you're going through."

Yeah, right, I was thinking.

"No, seriously. I know that you lost your father a couple years back. I, too, lost my father when I was about your age. It's a very confusing loss. I went through a tough, tough period. Fighting, drinking, getting kicked off the soccer team, breaking into an electronics warehouse and stealing some stuff. Fell in with a bad crowd." He rolled up his sleeve, showed me a crude tattoo. "That's what you do in the joint," he said. "A guy takes a needle and pokes holes in you and spreads ink on your arm. Hurts like hell. But you got nothing better to do."

"Yes, sir."

"That what you want to do with your life, son? Sit around in the joint while some idiot with a swastika tattooed on his forehead sticks holes in your arm?"

"No, sir."

"Didn't think so. I can tell you're a smart kid. Save yourself going through what I went through. I eventually attended an

Ivy League university, got a law degree from Yale—everything worked out. Now I own a company that's worth five hundred million dollars. But it was a nasty struggle getting there. Trust me. What you want to do, you want to stick with the program, keep your DRs to a minimum, suck it up, take it like a man. Pretty soon? Hey, you'll be going to college, dating a cute girl, studying hard, back on track to have a nice life."

"Thank you, sir."

Mr. Shugrue smiled, rolled his sleeve back down, and buttoned the cuff. I could feel the wine moving around in my veins. It made me feel all goofy and lazy. But even so, I could see something behind that smile, something dark and predatory in those eyes. "Well, I know you need your beauty sleep, son." He stood and walked over to the sideboard, picked up whatever it was that he'd been reading when I entered the room. "Just a little housekeeping to take care of before you go. A couple of admission forms to sign, whatnot, we'll have you out of here in a jiff."

I don't know why, but all of a sudden it was like I could feel Mike's forearm on my throat again. *Don't sign anything.*

"Sign?" I said.

Mr. Shugrue still had the broad smile on his face as he slapped a bunch of papers down in front of me. "Just a formality," he said.

I looked at the forms. There was a lot of little bitty writing on them, and a bunch of Post-it note sort of things with red arrows on them sticking out of the edges of the papers.

"What exactly are these?" I said.

"Oh, you know . . ." He waved his hand like he was shooing away a fly. "Just boring old yadda-yadda-yadda-type stuff. Liability waivers, admission forms, your eyes would glaze over in a heartbeat if I even told you. Just sign next to each of the little red arrows."

I kept sitting there. "Uh. Shouldn't, like, my mom sign these? Or something?"

Mr. Shugrue's smile faded slightly. "Sure, of course, she's already signed her forms. This is just the usual BS for the lawyers to file away in a drawer somewhere."

I scratched my head, reached out to look at one of the forms. It said DURABLE POWER OF ATTORNEY at the top. At the bottom was a Post-it note with a red arrow on it pointing at a little signature line with my name next to it. I flipped to the next sheet. It said something about RE: OSWALD TURNER, ADMINISTRATION OF TRUST FUND at the top. I squinted at it, reading, trying to make sense of what the thing was all about.

Martin Shugrue grabbed the forms and pulled them back. "Hey," he said. "You want to be a jailhouse lawyer, no problem, nobody's forcing you to sign."

"Can I see them, please?" I said.

His smile went away completely. "Rule One," he said. "Questions are disrespectful."

"I just feel like I should—"

Mr. Shugrue clapped me on the shoulder. "Knew a lot of guys like you in the joint," he said. "Thought their way right into prison." He stood. "Don't you worry about those forms, *Oswald*." Giving it a little twist as he said my name. Just like Don Guidry always did when Mom was out of the room.

"You go on back to bed," he said. "We'll take care of your paperwork at a later time."

Then suddenly he seemed like maybe he was worried he was coming off like a jerk, so he gave me this big smile and he said, "Hey, kid. You need anything, you just give me a call, huh?" And then he handed me a card. It said:

SUNVEST INDUSTRIES

MARTIN R. SHUGRUE
PRESIDENT

6699 BUFORD HIGHWAY
ATLANTA, GA 30010
770-555-1700

Something's not right, Dad. Trust fund? What's up with that? I don't have a trust fund! God, that's ridiculous. So why are they having me sign something that makes it sound like I do?

> Love,
> Oz

seventeen

Dear Dad,

After I was done with Mr. Shugrue, I went back to our dorm room and fell asleep. The plan was for us all to get up at about midnight and go down to work on the airboat. Any earlier and we risked getting caught by Coach Bell or the night watchman. Everybody agreed that the night watchman nodded off after Coach Bell went to bed, though, so once he was asleep we could go safely.

Boy, did I not want to wake up when the time finally came. Farhad shook me until my head about fell off, but I just kept lying there.

Mike was scowling at me. "Just leave him here," he said. "We don't need this kid anyway."

"Hey," I said. "I'm *coming*."

"Go ahead," Randall said, "sleep, dude. You're just gonna get in the way."

Randall seemed to parrot everything Mike said.

"Who made you such an asshole?" I said.

Meanwhile Mike was lowering a big red steel box full of tools out the window by the rope made from a braided sheet. Somewhere along the way his grip slipped and the tools fell the last five feet. They made a huge jangling racket.

"*Oh* hell!" Emmit said.

Everybody froze. Mike looked out the window. "I don't see anybody," he said after a minute. "I'll go down and check around, make sure we didn't wake up the watchman."

He climbed down, peeped around the corner, gave us the thumbs-up. Then he picked up the red toolbox and started walking briskly across the yard. Sean wanted to go next. But he was so big, he had trouble getting out the window.

Meanwhile Mike had gotten about halfway across the weedy yard toward the woods.

Suddenly Sean froze.

"What?" Randall said after a minute.

"Coach Bell," Sean said.

We all crowded around the window and watched. On the far side of the quad, Coach Bell was walking swiftly toward our side of the building. He couldn't see Mike yet. His view was blocked by the maintenance shed. But in a few strides he would be around the corner and Mike would be dead meat.

"Mike!" Emmit stage-whispered. "Mike! Dude! Look out!" Any louder and Coach Bell would have heard him.

Problem was, Mike couldn't hear him either.

It was terrible. We just stood there helplessly, knowing what was about to happen. Mike kept walking. Coach Bell came marching around the corner and, bam, there was Mike right in front of him.

"Hey!" Coach Bell yelled. "Get over here."

Mike, instead, started to run. Unfortunately, with the tools in his hand, he couldn't run very fast. Coach Bell followed, quickly closing the gap. The big red toolbox slammed awkwardly against Mike's leg, clinking and jangling with each stride.

"Drop the tools!" Farhad hissed. "Drop the tools!"

Just as Coach Bell was about to close the gap between them, Mike finally did drop the toolbox. But by then it was too late. Coach Bell tackled him and they went down in a heap. Mike tried to fight, but Coach Bell was even bigger and stronger. Mike got in a couple of licks. Then suddenly the dogs were racing across the yard.

One of them jumped on Mike, grabbing his arm in its teeth. Another got his shirt, ripping it off his back.

"They're gonna kill him!" Sean said.

But just as quickly as they'd jumped on him, Coach Bell said: "Hold!" The dogs immediately let go and stood there staring at Mike, teeth bared. Mr. Pardee strolled up and looked down at Mike, who was lying on the ground holding his arm.

Mr. Pardee said something we couldn't hear.

Mike said something back, and the old man kicked Mike in the ribs. Mike looked like he was about to attack the old man, but then the dogs started to move toward him and Mike sagged to the ground.

Coach Bell grabbed him by his shredded T-shirt, yanked him to his feet. They started walking across the yard.

"He's screwed," Emmit said. "He's totally screwed."

"*We're* screwed, you mean," Farhad said. "Mike's the one who knew about mechanics."

"Plus," Sean said, "even if we could figure out how to fix the engine, we need those tools."

"Maybe they'll leave them," Emmit said.

Everybody was starting to walk away. The red toolbox lay on its side in the middle of the yard.

"Check it out!" Emmit said. "They're leaving the tools. We've still got a chance if we've got the tools."

Just at that minute, Mr. Pardee turned around, went back, and picked up the toolbox.

We stood there in gloomy silence, staring at the dark, empty yard.

"Well, so much for that," Farhad said. "We're stuck in this prison forever."

More silence.

Then Randall said, "Somebody narced him out."

Nobody said anything.

"Where did Coach Bell come from? Huh?" Randall looked around at the other boys. "He was too far away to have heard when Mike dropped the tools. So how did he know?"

"Who?" Farhad said. "Who's the narc?"

"We've been together for six months. All of us." Randall stared at me, eyes narrowed. "Except for him."

"Give me a break," I said.

"Think about it," he said. "We don't know anything about this kid."

I shot him a bird.

"Come on, guys," Sean said.

"What are you defending him for?" Randall said. "Sean, you're the one who spent half the night in the Silent Room because of him. Who told them about the Pop-Tart?"

"Well . . ." Sean said.

"And what was he doing over there at Mrs. Kinnear's all day?" Randall turned to me. "I think you're a rat."

Sean and Emmit and Farhad all looked at me for a long time. I could see them thinking about it. The doubt started welling up in their eyes.

"Guys!" I said. "Come on!"

Emmit looked at me for a minute. Then, finally, he said softly, "How *did* Coach Bell know?"

"I don't know."

He shrugged and turned away. Randall snorted, like: *See, I told you so.* Then he and Farhad turned away, too. Finally Sean turned away, climbed into his bed.

"I didn't do it," I said.

But nobody said anything.

I could see how it would unfold after that. The word would get around that I was a rat for Mrs. Kinnear and nobody would even talk to me. There was this other kid, Smith—I don't even know if that was his first or last name—but everybody hated him. Supposedly Smith had ratted somebody out to Mrs. Kinnear. And now nobody would talk to him. I mean, nobody. He was like a ghost at the school, moving around, eating, sleeping, washing, dressing. And yet invisible.

I imagined what it would be like to be Smith. Stuck in this hellhole with no friends, nobody to talk to. However awful it was just being here, that would be ten times worse.

I lay in my bed staring at the bottom of the bunk above me. It was hot and muggy in the room, but I still felt cold. I could tell nobody else was sleeping either.

We'd all gotten psyched up, fooling ourselves that maybe we'd get out of here. And now everybody thought I'd stolen the dream from them.

Finally something struck me. I sat up.

"You think I'm a rat?" I said.

Nobody said anything.

I went to the window, looked out. There was nothing moving in the dark. I reached in my pocket. I could feel the key that Camryn had given me, a hard little metal thing, warm as skin.

"Well, I'm not," I said. "And I'll prove it."

Then I climbed out the window.

Am I crazy, Dad? When I was a kid, you were my hero. I knew other kids who always had posters on the wall of Power Rangers and all that stuff. But not me. I didn't need anybody to look up to besides you.

So would you have climbed out that window? Risked the dogs and Coach Bell and the gators and whatever else? I don't know. I wish I could ask you.

Love,

Oz

eighteen

Dear Dad,

I bet *you* never broke into anybody's house, did you? I mean, if you have the key, maybe it's not really breaking in. But it sort of is, wouldn't you say?

I went tiptoeing past the maintenance shed, then past the classroom building and up to the door of Dr. Kinnear's house. Then I stood there. My heart was beating so hard, I thought for a second that I might faint. But then I thought about what it would be like to be Smith, to be a ghost walking around here that nobody would talk to, and I put the key in the lock, twisted it, and walked in.

The Kinnears' house was very dark at night. No night-lights, no nothing.

I let my eyes adjust. Eventually I could make out the outlines of furniture. Not clearly . . . but clear enough to not bang into anything. I made my way to the stairs, taking one step, stopping, taking another step, stopping, waiting, listening.

Nothing happened.

I reached the stairs, began climbing up. It was an old house and every stair squeaked loudly. No matter how hard I tried, it didn't matter. SQUEEEAK! Then I'd wait, my heart pounding, expecting Mrs. Kinnear's bedroom door to fly open. Eventually, I'd move again. SQUEEEEAK! It was about the most nerve-racking thing I'd ever done in my life.

But then, suddenly, about halfway up the stairs, I got this feeling of excitement. In a weird, twisted kind of way, suddenly it seemed fun. I was putting one over on the evil Mrs. Kinnear. And she didn't even know it.

SQUEEEAK!

SQUEEEEAK!

Finally I made it. I was on the second floor. I could hear someone snoring softly in Mrs. Kinnear's bedroom. I walked slowly to Camryn's door, stood there for a minute.

What if Camryn screamed? What if she freaked out? I could probably get charged with attempted rape or something. However terrible this place was, I didn't want to end up in some juvenile prison either, getting beat up by gangbangers from Atlanta.

Finally, though, I twisted the knob, and walked into Camryn's room.

The first thing I noticed was the smell. It was a nice smell. A girl smell. I realized I hadn't smelled anything like that in a long time.

I tiptoed across the room, stood over Camryn's bed, looking down at her. She had a night-light, so I could see her face. She was even prettier than I remembered. Suddenly I got this kind of woozy feeling. The same feeling I used to get when Natalie Winters walked into the room back in eighth grade. I was *so* nuts about Natalie Winters. I never talked to her, never even told anybody else about it. But when she moved away last year I felt like . . .

Well, anyway, I don't mean to be getting all queer. All I'm saying is, Camryn had that effect on me.

And now I was thinking, *What now?* I didn't really want to touch her. That would be a little creepy. But if I tried to wake her up by making a noise, I might wake up everybody in the house. And turning a light on wasn't a good idea.

Before I could decide, she suddenly stiffened and gasped. Her eyes blinked open and I could see her staring up at me.

"Please," she whispered. "Don't hurt me."

"It's me," I said. "Oz."

Her body slowly relaxed and then she grabbed her pillow and hit me with it. "You asshole!" she whispered. "God, you about gave me a heart attack!"

Then she reached over and turned on the light on her bedside table. I looked around the room. Computer, desk, dolls, a poster of this boy band that had been popular back in seventh grade.

Camryn looked at me with a slightly wicked smile. "You *are* a bad boy," she whispered. "What are you doing here?"

"You gave me a key," I said.

She cocked her head. "I did, didn't I?" She pulled the covers up over her T-shirt. "I stole it from Mommy Dearest. It's some kind of passkey. It opens every single door on campus. Maybe we should go exploring." She kept watching me with her odd black eyes, this little smile hanging there on her face. "Or, like, maybe we should just explore something right here." Then she kind of pulled the covers down a little and scooched over in the bed.

I blinked.

"Well?" she said finally. "Are you gonna get in? Or not?"

I don't know what I'd expected. But not this.

"Uh . . ." I said. "I'd really like to. But actually I was hoping you could help me."

She kept looking at me. Then her face tightened. "Excuse me for thinking maybe you liked me or something."

"I *do*!" I said.

She scowled. "Yeah, sure."

"No, I'm serious. It's just . . . I need . . ."

"You need what?"

"Some tools."

She stared at me for a long time. "You snuck into my bedroom in the middle of the night because you want *tools*? Tools! God, I must really be losing it."

I started to explain what I needed them for, but she shook her head. "No, no, no, I don't want to hear it."

"Seriously," I said, "I really like you. It's just—"

"Turn around," she said brusquely.

"Huh?"

"Turn around. I need to put my pants on."

"Oh." I blushed. "Sorry."

I turned around, heard the rustle of cloth as she pulled on a pair of jeans.

She walked to the door, still buttoning her jeans. I couldn't help noticing she didn't have a bra on under her T-shirt. And the T-shirt was pretty thin. For a minute I was thinking, okay, screw the tools. But by then it was too late.

She held up her finger to her lips. "I don't have to tell you my stepmom will kill you and me both if she catches you here."

I nodded.

"Dad's tools are up in his office."

With that she turned off the light and opened the door.

We walked slowly up the stairs to the third floor. The ceiling was so low that I bumped my head. We both froze. The snoring in the other room stopped for a minute. My heart started slamming in my chest. Then the snoring started again.

"She snores like a cow," Camryn said.

I had assumed that it was her father. I tried to imagine the elegant Mrs. Kinnear snoring. I almost started laughing.

We padded slowly on up to the third floor, down a short hallway, and through a door.

"We can talk up here if we're quiet," she said, flipping on the light. I looked around. There was a large wooden desk on one side of the small room. The entire room was lined with books. Camryn walked across the room, pointed to a shelf full of large hard-backed books. "Dad wrote all of these. Before he got sick."

"What's wrong with him?" I said.

"He's got idiopathic neuropathy."

"What's that?"

"It's a degenerative disease that affects the nervous system." She ran her finger along the spines of all the books. "You know, he was one of the best known psychologists in the country. Before he got sick."

I walked over and started to pull one of the books out.

Camryn reached out and touched the back of my hand. Her skin felt hot.

"Don't. My stepmother is a neat freak. If she saw one of those books out of place, she'd freak out. She doesn't even want *me* in here."

"Why not?"

Camryn shrugged. Her thin T-shirt rode up and down over her nipples.

"Then again," I said, "maybe I wouldn't mind messing around after all."

"Ha," she said. "You blew your chance. You want tools? There're your tools." She opened a closet door. There on the floor was a large toolbox.

I opened the box. Inside was a set of gleaming tools, carefully packed, everything in order. Socket wrenches, screwdrivers, gap testers, all kinds of stuff.

"So you know about my dad," she said. "What does your dad do for a living?"

"He's dead," I said.

"Oh. Sorry."

"That's okay." I kept looking through the tools. "He was an inventor."

"An *inventor*. That's kind of cool. What did he invent?"

"Mostly he made gizmos for souping up cars. Cams, superchargers, stuff like that."

She looked at me blankly. "Like, uh, like on that TV show *Monster Garage*?"

"Well, sort of. Before he died we lived out on a farm in the country in Virginia. He had a whole machine shop out behind the house. Lathes, mills, drill presses, you name it. He could make anything. He used to let me hang out with him, help him out in his shop."

"So what are you gonna do with the tools?" she said.

I smiled. "We're gonna escape."

Her eyes widened. Then she got a wicked grin on her face. "Dude!" she said. "That *rocks*. How you gonna do it?"

I was about to answer when I heard a door slam underneath us. Then footsteps coming up the stairs.

"Oh no!" Camryn said. "Get in the closet!"

I got in the closet and closed the door just in time to hear the door of the office bang open.

"What on earth is going on?" It was Mrs. Kinnear.

"Huh?" Camryn said.

"Who were you talking to?"

"What do you mean, who was I talking to?"

"I distinctly heard voices."

"Look around. Do you see anybody that I could be talking to? I was singing to myself."

"No you weren't."

"What, you want to look in the closet? Huh? See if I'm hiding somebody in there?"

There were coats hanging in the closet. I didn't think they'd cover me enough to hide me if anyone opened the door. But I burrowed into the back of the closet anyway.

"Go ahead, check, dude!" Camryn said. "No, here I'll do it myself." I heard her hand rattle the doorknob.

Then I heard a flat smack, flesh against flesh. "Call me 'dude' again and you'll get worse than that," Mrs. Kinnear said.

"Ow! God!"

Another smack. "There. That's for taking the Lord's name in vain."

"You don't even believe in God."

SMACK! "That's for disrespecting me." There was a long pause. "Anything else? Hm? Any more editorials you'd like to offer up? No? Good. Then go to bed."

The door slammed and Mrs. Kinnear's footsteps thumped back down the stairs. I could hear Camryn sniffling.

I waited a minute and came out. Tears were running down her cheeks. I put my arms around her and gave her a hug. She sagged against me.

I had this weird feeling, like I was looking down at myself, like this was all happening to somebody else.

Finally she straightened up. "Wait about half an hour so she can fall asleep," she whispered to me. She put her lips right up against my ear, so close I could feel her breath on my skin. "Then let yourself out."

She looked into my eyes for a second, then kissed me on the lips. She looked like she wanted to kiss me more, but then she just walked to the door. She gave me a long look, with this really sad expression. Then she was gone.

Half an hour later I was underneath the window of our room. The rope had been pulled back into the room, so there was no way for me to get back in. Or to let the guys in the room know I had gotten some tools. I thought about it for a minute. The window was open because we didn't have air-conditioning. I threw a small wrench through the open window. It clanged around inside the room.

"What the—" I couldn't tell whose voice it was. But a

couple seconds later Sean and Emmit were looking out the window.

I held up the toolbox. Emmit stared at me for a minute, then grinned.

Sean and Emmit disappeared for a second, then I heard some arguing. I could tell that Randall was arguing against coming. But after a while everybody started climbing down the rope. Everybody except Randall.

"Randall's not coming," Farhad said.

"He still doesn't trust you," Sean said.

"That's his problem," I said. "Let's go find that boat, huh?"

We walked quickly to the tree line, then headed into the dark woods. It took about five minutes to get to the airboat. I hadn't had much of a chance to look at it the last time we were here. There was a bright moon tonight, so I could see it better. The pontoons were sunk deep in the mud and there were vines growing all over it.

"So you got tools," Farhad said when we reached the boat. "That's great and all. But Mike knew stuff about engines. We don't know squat."

"My dad was an automotive engineer," I said. "I used to help him work on engines all the time."

Farhad shrugged. "Okay. If you say so."

"Hey," Emmit said. "First thing we got to do is drag this thing out of the mud. If we don't get that done, it doesn't matter if the engine starts or not."

"Good point," Farhad said.

I set the toolbox down and everybody started coming up with brilliant ideas about how to get the boat out. Sean said we should use an engine hoist.

"Where we gonna get an engine hoist?" Emmit said.

"Uh . . ."

"We need ropes," Farhad said. "Except, dude, I'm not getting in the water with all those alligators and water moccasins."

"What we need is a bulldozer," Emmit said.

"Guys! Guys!" I said. "We don't have an engine hoist or ropes or bulldozers or anything else. We don't even have a shovel. The only thing we have is water."

The guys stared at me. "Water?" Sean said. "So what?"

I pointed at the airboat. There were a couple of old gas cans attached to it. "We get those gas cans, cut the tops off, fill them with water, pour the water on the mud around the pontoons. We stir it up with sticks until it liquefies, then we wash it away."

The other guys looked at one another. "It might work," Emmit said.

"We're gonna get dirt all over us," Farhad said. "You think they won't figure it out when laundry day comes?"

"So we take off our shoes and socks and roll up our pants. All we have to do is wear the same pants every night and then let them dry out during the day," I said.

"This is gonna suck," Farhad said.

"You got a better idea?"

The other guys were silent.

So we started working. The theory was okay. The mud around the pontoons didn't have any rocks in it or anything. It was just slimy silt. But still it was hard work dragging all the water up in the cans over and over and over. Farhad made comments the whole time and Sean kept falling in the mud and Emmit cut his hand pretty badly where we'd cut the top off of one of the gas cans. But we made progress. Slow progress.

By the time the horizon started lightening up we had one pontoon completely freed and the other partially finished. We were exhausted, muddy, mosquito-bitten, and frustrated.

We trooped back toward the building in silence, climbed back up into the room with about ten minutes to spare to get showered before PT started. Farhad and Emmit and I all showered. As we were showering, I looked around and wondered where Sean was.

When we went back to the room, I found out: Sean was sound asleep in the middle of the floor, still covered with grime. "Oh no!" Emmit said.

The amplified bugle sounded over the intercom, signaling it was time for PT.

"What are we gonna do?" Farhad said.

"Leave him," Randall said.

"But—" Emmit said.

I shook him, trying to wake him up, but it didn't seem to do any good. Randall scowled, then ran out of the room.

"Let's wait till the hall's empty, then drag him down to the showers," I said.

"I'll bring a change of clothes."

We waited until the noise of kids running had stopped, then we dragged Sean down the hallway on the slick linoleum. He didn't even stir. When we stuck him under the shower and turned on the cold water full blast though, he sat up, eyes wide, and starting howling and cussing.

"Get dressed!" Farhad yelled, throwing his clean outfit on the floor.

Then we sprinted out the door just in time for roll call.

Coach Bell was going through the names. When he got to Sean, he said, "Sean! Sean! Where's jelly-butt? Sean!"

Sean came stumbling out of the building at just that moment, hair wet.

"That's three extra miles!" Coach Bell yelled. "And no lunch today!"

Sean looked like somebody had kicked him in the stomach.

"Only five more days of this," I whispered to Sean as he got into line in front of me.

"I don't know if I can make it," he said.

So that's where it stands, Dad. Maybe we'll make it, maybe not.

Love,

Oz

nineteen

Dear Dad,

Well, next thing I know, I'm back over at the headmaster's residence working for Mrs. Kinnear again. Which was kind of good and kind of bad. The good thing was that I was in the house with Camryn. The bad thing was that all I did was work. I hadn't had any sleep at all, so I was in a daze and couldn't really concentrate all that well on what I was doing. And what did I have to concentrate on?

Mrs. Kinnear gave me another printed checklist for cleaning her room. It included directives such as the following:

All the ruffles on the coverlet of Mrs. Kinnear's bed had to touch the floor. But if they *dragged* on the floor, you got yelled at. As best I could tell, the difference between "touching" and "dragging" was about a millimeter.

The bedside table must be moved and vacuumed behind. But when you put the table back, the table had to be exactly three and one half inches from the wall. If it was three and a quarter inches, you got yelled at and told you were stupid and lazy.

You had to vacuum all the pictures. But if you accidentally made one crooked, you got yelled at.

Get the idea?

When I vacuum my own room, it takes about five minutes. It took two hours to vacuum Mrs. Kinnear's bedroom because of all these little details that you had to get right. On the bright side, though, I learned a lot of new words for "stupid." For instance, "cretin" and "troglodyte." That was in addition to all the usual words like "idiot," "moron," "fool," "jerk," "imbecile," and a bunch of cuss words.

When I was done with the work, Mrs. Kinnear made me check off each item on the page of cleaning requirements and then put my initials next to each check mark.

Around eleven o'clock Mrs. Kinnear finally left the house and stopped torturing me. As soon as she was gone, Camryn came out of her room.

"I thought she'd never leave," Camryn said. "Want to come help me, uh, clean my room?"

I was a little worried about not getting all my work done. Mrs. Kinnear had left me a three-page list of stuff I was supposed to get finished by the end of the day. "Uh . . ." I said.

"Well, if that's how you feel." She started to go back in the room.

"Hey, wait!" I followed her into her room.

The first thing she did was she started kissing me. I kissed this girl last year at a party once—Emma Tollberger. But, boy, it wasn't anything like this. Emma Tollberger was all nervous and kept pulling away from me and giggling. Not Camryn. She just shoved her tongue right between my teeth, then we sort of fell on the bed and rolled around.

Anyway, we kissed for a while and then I guess we finally got worn out, and so we just sat on the bed and talked. For however long it went on, I almost forgot how crappy my life was. I mean when a really cute girl wants to kiss you, a whole lot of other things can go wrong, and life still seems okay.

Eventually Camryn went downstairs to get us some lunch. She told me I should stay upstairs just in case Mrs. Kinnear came back.

While I was sitting there on Camryn's bed, I stuck my hands in my pockets and stared at the ceiling. I could tell I was about to fall asleep. But as I was lying there, I felt something in my pocket. I pulled it out. It was the business card Mr. Shugrue had given me. I thought about it for a minute. What was that guy's deal? Why was he getting me to sign a bunch of papers about some trust fund that I didn't even have?

I looked over at Camryn's computer. There was Hello Kitty staring at me from the screen. It seemed kind of odd. Camryn didn't seem like the Hello Kitty type. As I was staring at the computer, something suddenly occurred to me. I plopped down in the chair, logged on to the Internet, and Googled some words. *Martin Shugrue Sunvest Industries.*

I was puzzled to see that there was nothing on the Web that mentioned them. I didn't know much about companies . . . but I figured any guy who owned a company that was worth five hundred million dollars would be mentioned somewhere on the Web. But there was nothing at all. There was a Martin Shugrue, attorney at law, in Anchorage, Alaska, but I pulled up his Web site and he was an old fat guy. There was a Shugrue Tires in Seattle that was in the "fleet tire sales" business—whatever that was. The site showed a picture of the vice president of sales, who was a skinny blond guy named Martin "Kenny" Shugrue.

And that was about it.

I looked for Sunvest. Nothing.

I tried Martin Shugrue again. This time, way down on the list, I noticed a legal announcement.

ATLANTA, GEORGIA. FILING FOR CHANGE OF NAME, FULTON COUNTY, GEORGIA. ABEL DEWAYNE FELDER APPLYING FOR CHANGE OF NAME TO MARTIN R. SHUGRUE. It was dated about two years ago. I clicked on the link, but there wasn't any further information there.

Weird.

So I typed in "Abel Dewayne Felder" and hit the Enter key.

What popped up was a bunch of legal stuff, court records from all over the country. I couldn't really figure it out, but they were all like, ACE CREDIT VS. ABEL DEWAYNE FELDER. JUDGMENT FOR PLAINTIFF, $14,359. I mean, reams of this stuff. Like I said, I couldn't tell what it meant, but it looked like Abel Felder had gotten sued about a million times, and it looked like he'd lost every suit. I got the impression that he must have borrowed money from people and then never bothered to pay them back.

I kept working my way down the list and finally I found something different. It was a newspaper article from a paper in Idaho. The headline was: THREE SOUGHT IN MYSTERIOUS DISAP-PEARANCE.

I clicked on the link, found an article about how the founder of some kind of charity group had disappeared.

"In the wake of the disappearance of its founder, Albert J. Parker, three former employees of the Parker Foundation for Child Health are being sought for questioning by Green County Sheriff's investigators. As has been reported, the foundation had been under recent scrutiny for financial irregularities.

"Parker's blood-stained Jeep Cherokee was found three days ago. Mr. Parker, who had been in ill health for several years, was the founder of the Parker Foundation, which ran a camp for children with cancer in the mountains of Idaho.

"According to sources inside the foundation, three employees of the foundation had more or less wrested control of the group from its ailing founder. Some of these sources allege that the three had diverted foundation funds for their own enrichment.

"The three Parker Foundation employees sought in the case are Abel Dewayne Felder, Alexandra Felder, and Memluk Sezer."

There were several more articles following up on the story. They never found Albert Parker. But the next day they found a bunch of empty graves. No one was in them. But, as the sheriff pointed out, "You don't dig graves for exercise." As I read through it, I started getting a terrible feeling. The whole thing had a familiar ring to it. It sounded all too much like what was going on at the Briarwood School.

At the end of the article there was a picture of two of the three people that the cops were looking for in the case—Abel and Alexandra Felder.

"Holy crap!" I said.

There on the screen were Martin Shugrue and Mrs. Kinnear. They had their arms around each other, smiling these big fake-looking smiles at the camera. If you didn't know better, you'd have guessed they were married. But then . . . *did* I know better?

I guess I'd been so intent on watching the screen that I hadn't paid attention to what was around me. Suddenly I heard a noise behind me.

"What do you think you're doing?!"

It was Mrs. Kinnear. Fortunately the screen was angled so she couldn't see the picture of herself. I clicked on the exit box and stood up.

"I was just . . ."

"You were just *what*?"

She moved across the room real fast, whipped the computer screen around. There was nothing there but a picture of Hello Kitty.

"All e-mail programs here are password protected," she said. "So don't bother trying to e-mail Mommy."

She narrowed her eyes. "Get back to work!"

Your son,

Oz

twenty

Dear Dad,

We all set our alarms for midnight. But when they went off, none of us wanted to get up. For a while, we just lay there. Then, just as I was about to fall asleep, I had an image of something. It was a picture from one of the stories I'd read: a row of empty graves on the edge of a mountain in Idaho.

I hadn't had a chance to read any more articles about Albert J. Parker, the founder of the Parker Foundation. But I was pretty sure things hadn't ended well for him.

And I didn't want to end up like him.

I got up, started shaking everybody. They all grumbled and whined, but ten minutes later we were in our muddy clothes, climbing out the window. Even Randall came this time.

Mike didn't come, of course, because he was still gone. Gone where? Was it to this Silent Room place that everybody seemed so hesitant to talk about? I just didn't know.

.   .   .

It was a gloomy night. There was a little bit of moon, but it kept getting covered over with clouds, and patches of thick fog were rising off the black greasy-looking surface of the lake.

We started clearing muck from under the second pontoon of the airboat. For some reason there were more sticks, more roots, more snags under this one, and the work was slower going. Everybody started bickering and complaining. Randall said Sean wasn't working, and Sean complained that Farhad was splashing him intentionally, and Emmit kept saying the water was too cold.

About three o'clock in the morning everybody just sort of quit.

It was real quiet for a minute and then we started looking at each other.

"Screw this, man," Randall said. "It's not worth it."

Nobody else said anything. But I could tell they were thinking the same thing he was.

"We have to keep working," I said.

"For what!" Sean said. "It's gonna take us another night to get this thing moved. And then what? That gives us like four days to get the motor running. We don't have any parts; we don't know what we're doing; we don't have a battery; we don't have gas; and we don't know how to drive this thing. And if we *do* get it going and figure out how to run it—then what? We get lost out there in the swamp somewhere and end up dying of starvation or getting eaten by gators."

I started working again, carrying the water can up to the boat, dumping it, jabbing and stirring at the mud. We still had about six feet of pontoon stuck before we'd even have a prayer of moving the boat. I was stabbing and hacking at the mud and everybody was just sitting there watching me. I went to get another can of water, slipped in the slimy mud, fell down up to my neck in the muck.

Randall started laughing. "You're pathetic, Oz," he said.

I didn't say anything. I just got up and started working again. It seemed like every time I got some mud freed up, it just washed right back to where it had been. I had this horrible feeling of frustration. Almost claustrophobia. Like when Don Guidry would pin me on the floor in the basement and then whisper all this stuff in my ear.

After a minute Randall stood up.

"I'm out of here," he said, and started walking back into the woods.

I stopped working, looked at Sean. He looked at the ground. I turned to Farhad. He looked away. So did Emmit. I jabbed at the mud with my stick, felt something stab into my hand. I lifted my hand, saw a huge splinter sticking out beneath my thumb. It was probably an inch into my skin. Blood started dripping down my hand.

While I was staring at the blood, the other guys all turned and started walking away. Randall was already disappearing into the mist.

"Wait!" I called. "There's something you guys need to know!"

I heard Randall's voice. "It's over, dude."

"Come back," I said. "Before you leave, there's something I have to tell you."

Emmit turned and looked at me. His face was barely visible in the dark, but I could see how worn-out and dejected he was just from the way he was standing.

"Hold up," Emmit said finally. "Let's hear what he has to say."

I heard all the footsteps stop and then finally they filed back toward me. Randall stopped, folded his arms, stared down at me. "Okay. What?"

"There was this guy out in Idaho. His name was Albert Parker. He ran this camp for kids with cancer."

"So *what*?" Randall said.

"Just listen." I tossed the gas can on the ground. "About five years ago, Albert Parker hired a couple named Alexandra and Abel Felder. She was his secretary and he was the accountant for his foundation. Then, a short time after they were hired, Parker got sick. He stopped being able to do much and Alexandra and Abel stepped up to the plate. In fact, they pretty much took over the camp. Then they started raising lots of money. Going around the country telling rich people about all the fabulous stuff they were doing for these sick kids.

"Somewhere along the way there were some reports about how kids weren't getting their medicine and stuff. A couple of kids died who maybe shouldn't have. Meantime Alexandra and Abel Felder set up this big fund-raising shindig. They invited all these people from all over the country to come out and pledge money to the camp. They explained how they had all these big plans and how they were going to build all these big buildings and do all this great stuff. And all these rich people ponied up all this money at this big event. They raised over a million dollars in one day."

Randall sighed loudly. "Dude, I'm tired. Get to the point."

"The day after the big fund-raising event, Albert Parker's truck was found about two miles from the camp. Blood all over the seats. And guess where the Felders were?"

Nobody answered.

"The answer is—gone." I looked everybody in the eye, one at a time. "Gone. Along with well over a million dollars."

Randall rolled his eyes.

"I saw a picture of Abel and Alexandra Felder. Two years ago Abel Felder legally changed his name to Martin Shugrue. And Alexandra Felder? Her name is now Mrs. Gwen Kinnear."

Nobody spoke. Everybody's eyes got wide.

"Let me ask y'all something," I said. "Do any of you guys have trust funds?"

Everybody frowned.

Emmit said, "My dad made a lot of money in the music business back in the eighties. When he got divorced from Mom, he put some of it in a trust fund for me so my mom wouldn't spend it."

Sean cleared his throat. "Uh. Well. My granddad was a pretty successful guy. He owned a copper mine in Colorado. He left me something. I don't really know the details. But I think there's some kind of trust fund, yeah."

Farhad said, "My dad was a big cheese in Iran before the Ayatollah took over. I guess he's got some money squirreled away for me somewhere."

I looked at Randall. He shrugged irritably. "Sure. Okay. Yeah, I have a trust fund."

"When I first got here," I said, "Mike told me not to sign anything."

"And?"

"Mr. Shugrue fed me this big old meal the other night, gave me a bunch of wine so I was all happy feeling, and then handed me this stack of admission forms to sign. I looked at one of them and it said something about a trust fund. I don't have a trust fund."

Suddenly the moon came out from behind a cloud. Randall's face looked very white.

"I signed those forms," Randall said.

"So did I," Sean said.

"Yeah, but they just said it was a bunch of . . ." Farhad's eyes narrowed. "Those *bastards*!"

The woods were silent, no noise but the lapping of tiny waves on the shore.

"So . . ." Sean said. "This big Parents Day thing next week?"

I nodded. "Yep," I said. "That's what I'm thinking. I bet it's going to be a fund-raising event. Just like at that camp out in Idaho. I bet they're going to squeeze a bunch of money from our parents. Maybe from some other rich people they've invited. And the next day? They're gonna walk away with all that money."

"Along with our trust funds," Randall whispered.

Everybody was motionless. The moon went back behind a cloud.

"Maybe we should just wait it out then," Emmit said.

"I forgot to mention," I said. "A few days later, they found four empty graves on the back of the property. There were four kids at that camp who had trust funds. It looked like they were getting ready to kill all the kids with trust funds. Maybe Mr. Parker interrupted them or something. I don't know. Point is, we're all in danger."

"So how do you know this?" Emmit said.

"I snuck onto a computer at the Kinnears', searched for Martin Shugrue . . ." I shrugged.

Randall walked over and picked up the gas can, filled it with water, then looked up at us. "What are you lazy jerks waiting on?" he demanded. "God! Let's get busy!"

And we did.

By dawn the boat was free. But we were too tired to move it.

Love,

Oz

twenty-one

Dear Dad,

I felt like I was sleepwalking today. I fell asleep in math; I fell asleep in American history; I fell asleep at lunch. None of my teachers seemed to care.

After lunch we had a break and I went outside to walk around and try to wake up. As I was walking across the quad, I saw a golf cart puttering down the road from the boathouse. In the back was a kid I'd never seen. Sitting next to him was Mr. Edson, the guy who had transported me down here—and the only decent adult I've met since I was taken away last week.

I don't know why—but something suddenly struck me: Mr. Edson used to be a police detective.

I watched him take the new student into the administration building. Poor kid. He looked totally shell-shocked. I wondered if that was how I looked. Probably so.

After a couple minutes, Mr. Edson came back out carrying

an envelope with him—his delivery payment from the school. I walked over to him and said, "Hi, Mr. Edson."

He kind of blinked then said, "It's . . . Oswald, right?"

"Uh-huh."

"You doing okay, son?"

"Sure," I said. "Just thought I'd let you know, you better cash that check soon."

His eyes narrowed slightly. "Oh yeah? Why's that?"

"Look," I said, "I know you probably think I'm a bad kid and all that. But do you think you could put all that aside for just a second and listen to me?"

I could see he was pretty suspicious. He looked around, then shrugged.

"You used to be a police investigator, right?"

He nodded.

"You have any free time this week?"

He seemed irritated. "Look, what's this about?"

I grabbed his wrist, took out a pen and wrote "Alexandra and Abel Felder" on the back of his hand. I talked about how the school didn't feed people enough and how we were punished for all kinds of stupid things. Then once I'd gotten him interested, I explained what I knew about the Felders. If that was even their real names. "Anyway," I said finally, "I believe that Dr. Kinnear's life is in danger. Maybe mine and some of the other kids here, too."

I could see he didn't believe me. He kept looking over my shoulder like he was trying to find some excuse to bail on me.

"Just look them up on the Internet and look at their pictures," I said. "Abel Dewayne Felder and Martin Shugrue are the same guy. It'll take you five minutes. If I'm lying, you wasted five minutes. If I'm telling the truth . . . See, look, I'm just a kid. I don't know what to do. But you used to be a policeman, you'll know what to do."

"Sure, kid," he said. It was obvious he thought I was jerking him around.

"Five minutes," I said.

"I gotta go," he said. Then he stopped at the golf cart and said, "Son, fighting this place will only hurt you."

"I know you mean well," I said. "Otherwise I wouldn't have come to you."

As I was walking back to the school building, Mr. Pardee walked over to me and said, "What were you talking to that man about?"

"Pardon me, sir?" I said.

He grabbed my arm, about shook my teeth out of my head. "Don't act stupid. I saw you talking to him."

"I was just saying hello, sir."

"Well, don't!"

"Yes, sir," I said.

When I wasn't thinking about sleep, I was thinking about Camryn. I was afraid that her dad was in danger. If Mrs. Kinnear and Mr. Shugrue had killed this Albert Parker guy two years ago, they'd probably kill Dr. Kinnear, too. And if they killed Dr. Kinnear, they might kill Camryn.

I kept hoping to see Camryn, thinking maybe she'd come outside for exercise or something. But I never saw her. I tried to think of some sort of good reason for going over to the house. But I couldn't think of one. And if I went over there without a good reason and got caught, Mrs. Kinnear might stick me in the Silent Room with Mike.

Around three o'clock Mr. Akempis walked into English class with his usual sour expression on his face and said, "Oswald."

"Yes, sir?"

"Come with me."

My palms started to sweat. Nothing good could be happening here. I followed Mr. Akempis out the door, across the quad, and into the administration building. We went up the stairs and into Mrs. Kinnear's office. It was a very fancy place, all the furniture very expensive-looking. Behind the desk was a filing cabinet. Mrs. Kinnear was sitting at her desk looking busy with some paperwork.

"Sit," she said.

"Yes, ma'am." I sat. She kept diddling around, making me sweat.

Finally she looked up. "I just got a very disturbing phone call," she said.

My heart sank. I felt like I needed to throw up all of a sudden.

"Mr. Edson just called me. Do you want to know what he told me?"

I shrugged. My heart was banging away inside my ribs.

"He said that you told him some kind of cockamamie story about the school. He said you told him we were keeping kids prisoner here and abusing them and not feeding them enough and various other things."

I knew it wouldn't do any good to deny it. "Yes, ma'am," I said sullenly.

"Is that all you talked to him about?"

"Uh . . ." I looked at the floor.

"Don't lie to me!"

Was it possible that Mr. Edson hadn't told her about all my accusations? Maybe he'd thought what I said about Mrs. Kinnear and Mr. Shugrue being suspected murderers was so bizarre that he didn't even bother to tell her about it.

"Look," I said, "I don't think it's right for you to make me work at your house all day, miss school, and then not even feed me. Yes, ma'am, I did tell him about that."

"His cell phone cut off in the middle of our conversation. Are you sure that's all you told him?"

I tried to look confused. "What else would there be to tell him?"

Her eyes were narrow slits. She drummed her fingers on the table. "I'm going to get to the bottom of this."

I just sat there.

"Don't move," she said. "I need to do something."

She stood and walked out of the room. As soon as I heard her footsteps fade off down the hallway, I jumped up and went around her desk, tried the drawers of the filing cabinet. They were locked. I scrabbled in the drawer of her desk, found a key, unlocked the cabinet. Then I started rifling through the drawers. I wasn't sure what I was looking for. But I figured I'd know it when I got there.

In the bottom drawer, I found it.

A big fat file that said TRUSTS at the top. I pulled it out. There was one folder that said RANDALL CUMMINGS, one that said FARHAD KARROUBI, one that said MIKE SHEPHERD, one that said SEAN GRAINGER. And one with my name on it. I pulled mine out. Inside were a bunch of legal papers. I couldn't make any sense of them. There was lots of itty-bitty writing and all these words I didn't understand. At the bottom of the pile was a document that said: BENEFICIAL TRUST OF OSWALD TURNER.

Dad, I flipped through it and found your signature at the bottom.

How come I never heard anything about this, Dad? Do I have a trust fund? It's not like you were some rich guy. The whole thing doesn't make sense.

I stuffed the papers back in the filing cabinet, locked the cabinet just in time to return the key to the desk drawer and sit down.

I had gotten to the desk when I noticed something was out of place. I hadn't quite gotten one of the filing cabinet drawers all the way closed.

Mrs. Kinnear sat down and stared at me. "You're sweating, Oswald. Why is that?"

"It's hot, ma'am." I tried not to look at the filing cabinet.

"Well, I tried to call Mr. Edson again to get to the bottom of this. But lucky for you, his phone appears to be on the blink."

She kept looking at me.

"Meantime, dinner tonight is two biscuits and a vegetable. No meat, no dessert, no second helpings." She smiled. "And tomorrow you're cleaning my toilets again."

"Yes, ma'am," I said. I tried to look sullen about it. But cleaning toilets meant seeing Camryn again. Which seemed a pretty fair trade to me.

"Get out of my sight."

I stood and walked to the door.

"Hey!" She was pointing her finger at me. "I'm watching you. One slip and I'll take Mike out of the Silent Room and put you there instead."

Well, Dad, so now I know for sure where Mike is. I just don't know what it means.

Love,

Oz

twenty-two

Dear Dad,

We got up again around midnight, snuck out the window, and went down to work on the airboat. Sean was practically passing out, he was so tired. But he came anyway.

When we got down to the airboat it seemed like the mud had risen back up and sucked the whole boat down.

"Oh *no!*" Sean said.

"Hold on, hold on," I said. "Let's see what's going on."

It turned out that what looked like solid mud was actually fairly thin glop, about the consistency of hand cream. But it still took an hour of messy work to get rid of it all.

After that we got sticks from the woods and levered the airboat up onto the bank.

It was sort of like in those movies about making the pyramids. You'd go, "Heave! Heave! Heave!"—pushing until your arms were about to pop. And each time, the boat would move about an inch.

We were all watching the bank and heaving away when suddenly Sean went: "Oh my God."

Everybody stopped heaving. "What?" Emmit said.

Sean was wide-eyed, pointing at the ground.

We all came around to see what he was pointing at. There, on the ground, was a man.

A dead man.

Well, putting it another way, it was a skeleton. There was still a patch of black hair on its head, and it was dressed in green coveralls. Everybody stepped back.

Everybody except Randall. Who said, "Cool!"

Then he bent over and tugged on the sleeve of the skeleton. The skull fell off and rolled down the bank a couple of yards, lodging in the mud.

"Don't touch it!" Farhad said.

"How are we gonna get the boat up onto the bank if we don't move it?" Randall said.

Sean just kept staring.

"How long you think he's been here?" Emmit said.

"Years probably," I said.

"I wonder how he died?"

"Maybe the boat slipped over on him and crushed him."

I pointed at the fabric of the dead guy's coveralls. "What's that?" I said.

Everybody squinted at a small hole in the fabric.

"Looks like a bullet hole," Emmit said softly.

"We have to call the police," Sean said. His voice was all quavery.

"Oh, yeah, great idea, dude," Randall said. "Except all the

phones on campus are locked. And you need a special pass code to use them anyway."

"Well . . . then we've gotta tell Mrs. Kinnear. Or . . . or . . . somebody."

"Dude!" Randall said. "Earth to Sean! Somebody shot this guy. For all we know it was Mrs. Kinnear who did it."

"But—"

"He's right, Sean," Emmit said. "Much as it pains me to admit that Randall is right about anything . . ."

"Blow me!" Randall said.

"Guys, guys," I said. "Let's not get distracted here. We've got to move him and keep going."

"Maybe we could bury him and give him a little ceremony or something," Emmit said.

There was a long silence.

"Well, I'm not touching it," Farhad said.

"Me neither," Sean said.

I looked at Emmit and Randall. Emmit shrugged. "Hey, I don't care," Randall said. "I think it's cool."

"Yeah, 'cause you're sick," Emmit said.

I managed to avert a fight, and then we started moving the dead guy. It wasn't really like moving a dead person—more like a bag of bones. All the flesh had pretty much been eaten away, so the jumpsuit was the only thing holding it all together.

Randall picked up the skull, balanced it on his head, and said, "I am the ghost of the boat man! I have come to haunt you!"

"Could you possibly show a little respect?" Emmit said.

Randall kept clowning though. Finally we had all the bones piled up next to a tree.

"I'm gonna say a prayer," Emmit said.

Randall rolled his eyes. But when everybody bowed their heads, he did, too.

Emmit mumbled a few words that I couldn't really make out. And then we stood there for a second.

"We better get back to work," I said finally.

It took another hour or so to get the airboat all the way up onto the bank where it would be steady enough to work on the engine. This was our third night with no sleep and we were all pretty much dead on our feet.

"I can't take it anymore," Sean said. Then he sat on the side of the pontoon and immediately fell asleep, snoring loudly. After a minute he fell off the pontoon onto the ground. Everybody laughed. Except Sean. Sean just lay there snoring contentedly on the ground.

"What next?" Emmit said.

"The engine," I said. "We have to see if we can get it to run."

"Don't we need a battery?"

I nodded.

"Then how—"

"The golf cart," I said. "The one Mr. Pardee drives around in. We're going to have to steal a battery from it, then put it back each morning when we're done."

So we all trooped back to the campus—all of us except Sean, who was busy snoring away on the ground—and located the golf cart. It wasn't locked up or anything—just sitting out in the open next to the maintenance shed. I opened up the battery cover and found four rechargeable batteries on the cart, each the size of a car battery. I unhitched the wires from one of them.

"Who wants to carry it first?" I said.

Emmit shrugged. "I guess I will." He picked it up. "Damn!" he said. "You didn't tell me it was gonna be so heavy."

We had to carry the battery in shifts. It must have weighed about fifty pounds. Which would have been bad enough anytime. But we were already exhausted. The adrenaline rush of finding the skeleton had lasted a few minutes. But by now it had worn off. Emmit and Randall kept bickering and Farhad kept saying we'd never make it, and I was starting to feel more and more like we'd never be able to get this done in time.

But finally we got there. Randall dropped the battery on the boat.

"Hey," Farhad said. "Where's Sean?"

We looked around. And sure enough, Sean was gone.

I felt the skin prickle on the back of my neck.

"Sean? Sean!" We couldn't call too loudly because they'd hear us back on the campus.

"Oh my God," Emmit said. "Look." Emmit was pointing at the water.

"What?" I said. All I could see was the oily black water.

Farhad came over and shined his flashlight on the muddy ground. There in the slick mud where the boat had been were a series of claw prints and a big S-shaped slash in the mud.

"Those are gator tracks," Emmit said.

"No they're not," Randall said.

"Yes they are!"

"No, dude, those are *huge* gator tracks," Randall said.

We went down and looked. The tracks came out of the water in one place. Then they went back in farther down the bank.

Nobody wanted to say anything. But we were all thinking it.

"What if he got eaten?" Farhad said finally.

"We gotta look for him," I said.

"Where?" Randall said. "If he's been eaten, there's nothing to find."

"Yeah, well, it could have like torn his arm off," Emmit said. "He could be bleeding in the bushes ten feet from here."

"Dude, if there's a gator out there big enough to eat Sean," Randall said, "then I don't feel like sticking around here. And if there's not, then I'm worn-out. Either way, I'm outta here."

Randall turned and walked away.

"Once again," Emmit said, disgusted.

"Let him go," I said. "We're all tired."

"What about Sean?"

"We'll find him," I said.

We searched up and down the edge of the lake. But there was no Sean.

At around five thirty, the sun started to come up. "We gotta go, Oz," Emmit said.

"Just ten more minutes."

"I'm not sticking around here," Farhad said.

"Just a couple more minutes!" I said. Sean had been decent to me when nobody else had. I felt like I owed it to him to find him.

"I'm going," Farhad said.

Emmit looked at the ground.

"Whatever," I said. I went back to searching the bushes. When I turned around, Emmit and Farhad were gone.

.　　.　　.

I never found Sean. And I was late for PT.

Coach Bell saw me walking out from behind the maintenance shed. My shirt was dirty and there was a streak of mud on my pants. I ran over and got in line with the other boys.

Coach Bell sauntered over and looked me up and down, this big sarcastic grin on his face. "Gosh, Oswald, it's real nice of you to grace us with your presence."

"Yes, sir!" I said, staring straight ahead.

He plucked at my T-shirt with the tips of his fingers. "That's two DR points for tardiness and two for grooming. Oh, gosh! No visits from Mommy! Not for a very, very long time."

"Yes, sir," I said. At this point I was too tired to care.

He walked around me in a slow circle. "You know where our fat little friend Sean is?" he said.

"No, sir."

"Because he's late for PT, too." He kept walking around and around me. I just stared straight ahead, like some marine in boot camp. "I wonder if the two of you were up to something together."

"No, sir."

"Well, maybe a ten-mile run would help your memory."

"Ten miles? Sir?"

"Ten miles," he said. "Or four hours. Whichever comes first. No breakfast for you, my boy. But we wouldn't want you to starve. I'll let you stop for lunch. Then you can have a biscuit and some vegetables." He smiled. "*Cold* vegetables. From a can."

"Uh. I was supposed to clean Mrs. Kinnear's toilets today, sir," I said.

"Her toilets, huh?" This seemed to amuse Coach Bell. "I'll have a talk with her."

"Yes, sir."

He stared at me. "Well? What are you waiting on, doofus? Start running!"

I was already starving and totally exhausted. This was going to be horrible. I started to run, but Coach Bell reached out and grabbed my shirt, bunching it up in his fist. "Hey!" He yanked me toward him so my face was right up in front of his. "If you remember where Sean is, then I might think about letting you skip the ten-mile run."

"I don't know, sir."

"Then start running." He planted his foot on the seat of my pants and gave me a hard shove. I fell down in the dirt. Some of the kids laughed. It felt like everything was caving in on me.

For a minute I felt like just lying there. But finally I got up and started to run.

I'm trying, Dad. I'm really trying.

Love,

Your son,

Oz

twenty-three

Dear Dad,

I'll tell you something. After you've run ten miles and hardly eaten anything in two days, cold green beans are just about the best food in the world. The cafeteria lady, Mrs. Ellis, slipped me an extra can to go with my biscuit. It took me about two minutes to eat them all. Including the juice.

My legs were sore; my lungs were burning; one ankle felt all wobbly and weak. But I had this strangely pleasant feeling. I wasn't even tired, not right then.

So when Sean sidled up to me in the cafeteria, I didn't even jump.

"What happened to you?" I said.

"Check this out—" he said, grinning.

"Hold on," I said. "When did you get back?"

Sean shrugged. "After PT."

"I'm surprised they didn't make you run."

"I told them I was in the bathroom all during PT. I told them

I had diarrhea, that I pooped in my pants and stuff. Coach Bell was like, 'Too much information, lard-ass.'"

"We searched for you for two hours!" I said. "What did you do? If you just came back to the room and slept, I'm gonna strangle you."

"Nah, nah, nah. I'll tell you later." Then he got up and sort of bumped into me. I felt something fall into my lap. "Oops!" he said.

After he was gone, I looked down. There was a piece of fried chicken wrapped in a napkin lying in my lap. I stood up, put it in my pocket, started to walk out of the cafeteria. My stomach was grumbling.

"Hey!" Coach Bell yelled at me. "Where do you think *you're* going?"

"To class, sir."

"No you're not. You're on work detail. Mrs. Kinnear's toilets still need licking out." He seemed to find this very funny.

"I'll go there right away, sir," I said.

"You're dadgum skippy you will," he said.

Dadgum skippy? I thought. *What a douche bag.*

I headed over to the Kinnears' house, pausing behind the maintenance shed to gobble up the fried chicken Sean had slipped me. There were little pieces of lint and paper napkin sticking to it. But, man, it was better than anything I've ever eaten. Even better than cold green beans out of a can—if you can believe that.

As I was inhaling the chicken, I noticed the golf cart sitting next to the maintenance shed. I realized that in our concentration on finding Sean last night, we'd forgotten to bring back the battery. My heart sank. Mr. Pardee used the golf cart a lot. If he found the battery missing, there'd be hell to pay.

But there was nothing I could do about it now.

When I reached the door to the Kinnears' house, it opened and Mrs. Kinnear was staring at me with her cold green eyes. "You're late."

"Coach Bell made me run laps this morning."

"Get inside!" She pointed through the door.

When I got inside, she said, "Upstairs. Start cleaning the bathrooms, then I'll find something else for you to do." I started to walk away, then she said, "Wait!"

"Ma'am?"

"Your hands. Are they clean?"

"Uh. Yes, ma'am." I figured, how clean do they need to be to wash out a toilet?

Mrs. Kinnear looked at me suspiciously. "Hold them out," she said.

I held out my hands.

She walked over and felt my fingers. They were slippery with chicken grease. She moved closer, grabbed one finger so that her red-painted thumbnail was jabbing into it, and then lifted my hand to her nose. She took a deep breath, then smiled wickedly. "Did I not leave specific instructions?" she said. "You've been placed on our Special Needs diet. That means vegetables and bread only. And here you are eating chicken."

I didn't say anything.

"One of those other little snakes must have slipped you a piece." She dug her thumbnail in deeper. "Who was it?"

My eyes were watering.

"Who was it?"

I felt like screaming. But I couldn't give her the satisfaction.

"Alright then, fine," she said. "But you know, something just struck me. All those harsh abrasives ruin the porcelain in my toilets. I'll need you to clean them with your hands. No sponges, no toilet brushes. Nothing. Not even surgical gloves. Just these filthy, disgusting hands."

She gave my finger a last jab with her thumbnail, then dropped my hand.

"Yes, ma'am," I said.

I cleaned the toilets and I cleaned the tub and the shower. By the time I was done, my hands were like prunes. I kept hoping to see Camryn, but she stayed in her room playing old punk music really loud on her stereo.

Around three o'clock I saw something out the window that caught my attention. It was Mr. Edson, walking across the quad. Two things struck me. First was that he didn't have any kids with him. Second was that he wasn't on the golf cart. Which meant that Mr. Pardee had probably found that the battery was missing.

If Mr. Edson was here to see Mrs. Kinnear, I figured maybe the best thing I could do would be to catch him before he spoke to her, tell him I just made everything up and that he should forget I'd ever talked to him. Maybe if I begged him, he wouldn't tell Mrs. Kinnear about the information I'd dug up about her and Mr. Shugrue and the dead man out in Idaho.

I knew that Mrs. Kinnear was upstairs taking a shower, so I ran out onto the quad.

"Mr. Edson," I said. "Hey, Mr. Edson."

Mr. Edson looked around nervously. "Hey," he said. "Let's go over here. You probably don't want to be seen talking to me."

We stepped around behind a row of bushes near the maintenance shed. "Look, Mr. Edson," I said, "I'm sorry about the other day. I don't know what I was thinking. . . ."

He interrupted me. "I owe you an apology, son," he said. "How did you know about the check?"

"Huh?"

"The first thing you said to me was, 'You better cash that check soon.' Why did you say that?"

"Uh. Did I say that?"

His jaw clenched. "I'm sorry about calling Mrs. Kinnear." He looked around nervously again. "I hope I didn't get you in trouble."

"Well . . ."

"Look, that's beside the point now. The reason I'm here is that the check they gave me *did* bounce. After that happened I thought about what you said and just for the heck of it I poked around to see what I could find out about Martin Shugrue."

My eyes widened a little. "You found it, didn't you?" I said. "I was telling the truth about them killing that guy out in Idaho."

He cleared his throat. "They never found a body."

"Oh, come on!" I locked eyes with Mr. Edson.

After a minute, he looked away. "Okay, yeah. What you said . . . it seems possible that Shugrue and Mrs. Kinnear are doing something bad here."

"Then please, help us!"

He grimaced. "Look, I'm just a private citizen now. I could call the police here, but I don't think that if they came out here today, they'd find anything that would do you any good. So I called a friend of mine. He's with the FBI. He's going to come out here on some kind of pretext. If he finds that Mrs. Kinnear and Martin Shugrue are who we think they are, he'll take them down. Okay?"

I felt this huge sense of relief flow through me. The FBI! Wow. We were home free.

"I can't guarantee when he'll be out here," Mr. Edson said. "But his name is Special Agent Carl Suttles. He'll find you. Meantime you're just going to have to sit tight."

"Yes, sir," I said.

"I'm going to go over to the admin building and hassle them about the check they bounced. If they ask me about you, I'll minimize the whole thing, tell them I blew it out of proportion. Get on back to whatever you were doing."

I was imagining Mrs. Kinnear stepping out of the shower, looking out the window, and seeing me with Mr. Edson. "You don't have to tell me twice," I said.

"Remember. Special Agent Carl Suttles. If it's anybody else, don't talk to them." Mr. Edson shook my hand. "Stay strong, Oswald. You're gonna get out of this okay. I promise you."

"Thank you, sir."

I ran back to Mrs. Kinnear's house. Mrs. Kinnear was in the upstairs hallway wrapped in a very small towel. For a lady with a stepdaughter my age, she was not hard to look at. Most girls I knew would have traded bodies with her in a heartbeat. She turned around as soon as she heard my footsteps.

"What are you smirking at?" she said.

"Nothing, ma'am," I said.

"There's a ladder out back," she said. "Get on the roof and clean the gutters."

"Yes, ma'am."

Mrs. Kinnear got all dressed up and went over to the administration building after a while. When I was done with the gutters, I went inside. Camryn was sitting in the living room watching TV.

"I heard you working today," she said. "But I didn't want to come out until Queen Beast was gone."

"That was probably smart," I said.

"Come here," she said. "I want to show you something."

I followed her up the stairs, down the hallway. She opened the door of the bedroom at the end of the hall. Lying on a bed in the middle of a bare room was Dr. Kinnear.

"Hey, Dad!" she yelled loudly. "Dad!"

He didn't even stir.

She looked over at me, then walked over to the bed. There were all kinds of medicine bottles on the bed next to her sleeping father. She began hunting through them.

"So," she said, "I heard Gwen taking a shower. Did she do the drop-the-towel trick?"

"What do you mean?"

"When she's got boys over to help around the house, she likes taking a shower while they're standing around all sweaty-looking. Then she'll come out and accidentally-on-purpose drop her towel. Then when they stare at her, she'll go off on them like they're pervs. She does it to torture them."

"No, she didn't do that," I said. "But that teeny little towel didn't leave much to the imagination though."

Camryn snorted. Then she picked up a bottle of pills. "See this right here?"

She handed me the bottle. I read the label. "Protriptin," I said. "What's that?"

"I looked it up on the Internet. I'll tell you what it isn't. It isn't for what he's got. It's a very powerful antipsychotic drug."

I frowned. "You mean like . . ."

"I mean like it's something you give to schizophrenics. According to the stuff I read on the Internet, if you give it to a normal person, it makes them all groggy and messed up. Side effects include tiredness, nausea, weight loss, forgetfulness, and what they call 'decreased emotional engagement.'"

"What's that mean?"

"It means, basically, you stop caring about anything."

"Whoa. So you're saying . . ."

"Basically?" She nodded. "Yeah, that bitch is poisoning my father. It's no wonder she's got him under her control."

"I'm not surprised," I said. "I have some things to tell you, too."

"Like what?"

"Like, your stepmother is not who she says she is."

A line formed in the middle of Camryn's forehead. "What do you mean?"

I told her all about what she and Martin Shugrue—or Abel Felder or whatever his real name was—had done at the retreat for kids with cancer out in Idaho.

Camryn's jaw hardened. "Damn her."

"I know," I said. "But here's the thing, I think they're aiming to make a big haul on Sunday at Parents Day. My guess is that they'll skip out the next day."

Camryn grabbed the bottle off the nightstand. "We have to flush these."

"Wait," I said. "You know how your stepmother is. If you ditch them, she'll know you've figured out what they are. I bet she counts them every day."

"Yeah, but I've got to get him off these drugs so that by Sunday he'll be able to think straight."

I took the bottle from her, poured them out in my hand. "Look," I said. "Capsules. They're basically a pill-shaped skin with the medicine inside. We can pull them apart, empty each one out, and fill them with cornstarch or something. That way your stepmother won't know he's not getting drugged."

"Good idea."

"We better hurry before she comes back."

We ran down to the kitchen, started pulling the pills apart and pouring their contents down the drain.

"By the way," I said, "there is some good news. You know that guy Mr. Edson? The one who brings kids to the school?"

She nodded.

"He's an ex-cop. I told him everything I found out about your stepmom and Martin Shugrue."

Her eyes widened. "Are you nuts? He'll just go and tell Mom."

"Well, Mr. Edson tried to tell her. But he got cut off when he was calling her, and he only told her that I'd made some accusations about kids being treated badly here. Anyway, he looked into it a little and found out that I wasn't lying."

"Can you trust him?"

"I think so," I said. "He doesn't work directly for your step-mother. He delivers kids to a whole bunch of schools like this. I really think he believes places like this are good for messed-up kids. I mean, maybe some of them are."

"Well, what's he gonna do about it?"

"That's the good news," I said. "He's telling the FBI. He contacted this friend of his, a special agent named Carl Suttles." I held up one of the pills. "In fact, you ought to save one of these to show him. It'll prove that your stepmother is poisoning your dad."

"Good idea." Suddenly Camryn looked up and said, "Oh no! She's here."

I didn't have to ask who *she* was. The front door was rattling. "Take the pills!" I said. "I'll distract her."

Camryn grabbed the pills we'd been packing with cornstarch, then raced out of the kitchen and up the stairs. Meanwhile the front door was opening. I hurriedly replaced the cornstarch box in the cabinet above the sink. It had come from the very top shelf, so I had to climb up on the black marble counter to put it back. As I was climbing down, I noticed a dusting of cornstarch on the counter. But before I could do anything about it, Mrs. Kinnear swept into the room.

I was sure she would see the cornstarch.

"What are you doing?" she demanded. "Stealing food again?"

"No, ma'am. I was just—"

She waved her hand, her red fingernails almost grazing my face. "I don't really care," she said. "Do you know where the scotch is?"

"Excuse me?"

"Scotch. Whiskey. It's under the sink. I've had an extremely trying day, and I want a drink. Pour me a scotch and water. Then bring it up to my bedroom."

I had no idea how to make scotch and water. But she was gone before I could ask. So I got out a glass, put some ice in it, poured it half full of scotch, and then filled it the rest of the way with water.

I took it up to her bedroom, knocked on the door.

"Come!"

I walked in tentatively. She was sitting on her bed in a bathrobe. I was thinking, *This just keeps getting creepier and creepier.*

"I didn't say scotch on the rocks!" she snapped.

"I'm sorry. Do you want me to—"

"Oh never mind. Just put it right there."

I put it on her nightstand.

"Have you ever given a foot massage?"

"Uh. Not really."

"Well, you're about to learn."

She leaned back, closed her eyes, stretched out her feet, and waggled her toes. Her toenails, like her fingernails, were bright red. With her eyes closed, she didn't look nearly as mean. In fact, she looked like one of these movie stars in a film who wakes up all beautiful with her hair perfect, and her makeup in place.

As I was sitting down on the bed, Camryn walked by in the hallway and stuck her finger in her mouth and made a face like she was gagging. Then she made a motion like: *Oops! I just dropped my towel*—bending over all comically with her boobs and her butt sticking out. I really had to work hard to keep from busting out laughing.

So I tried to concentrate on poking around on Mrs. Kinnear's feet. Like I said, I'd never given a foot massage. Frankly, I hope I never will again. But I must have done something right, because Mrs. Kinnear didn't complain at all. In fact, after a few minutes, she started to snore.

Well, Dad, I learned one main lesson today. Sometimes really beautiful women have extremely stinky feet. Pretty profound, huh?

Love,
Oswald

twenty-four

Dear Dad,

After you've been awake pretty much continuously for three nights, you start feeling really weird. Especially after the sun goes down. I was basically okay during the day. But during supper the light was starting to get dim outside, and I literally fell asleep in my food. I'm talking like right out of *The Three Stooges*—face down into my biscuit and cold green beans. When I woke up, everybody was laughing and pointing at me. I felt pretty stupid.

I went back to my room and fell straight to sleep. As I was falling asleep, I saw Sean walk into the room. Somewhere in the back of my head I was wondering what had happened to him the night before. But I couldn't get up the energy to ask.

Next thing I knew somebody was shaking me and shaking me and shaking me. It took me a while to wake up. And I was in a really bad mood when I did. It was Emmit. I nearly hit him in the face, I was so mad.

Finally I woke up enough to realize there was no reason to be mad at him. But still I was not in the mood to be messing around in the swamp.

A few minutes later, though, we were down at the airboat. Randall had made himself useful—for once—and siphoned some gas out of the Jeep that Coach Bell drove around the island on, filled up three milk cartons with it.

"You sure you know what you're doing?" Randall said.

I ignored him as I poured the gas into the gas tank. Then I hooked up the battery, tried to crank the engine. As I expected, it didn't do anything.

"So what happened to you yesterday, Sean?" I said as I started checking things on the engine.

"Yeah," Randall said. "You scared the piss out of us. We were looking for you all night."

"*Some* of us were," Emmit said, giving a significant look to Randall.

Before Randall and Emmit could start getting into it, Sean said, "Man, you wouldn't believe—I was sleeping away down there and suddenly I feel somebody nudging me. I was like, 'Dude, go away! I'm sleeping!' But I kept feeling them. It was almost like they were lying on me. So I open one eye . . ." He looked around at us. "Guess who it was?"

Everybody shook their head.

"It was a gator. I mean, that thing made me look tiny. He was just lying there with his mouth half open, doing nothing, just breathing this dead-fish breath in my face."

"Whoa!" Farhad said.

"It must have been attracted to the heat," Emmit said.

"I don't care why it was attracted to me. It scared me to death! I mean that thing's teeth were like *this* far from my face." He held his fingers about a tenth of an inch apart. "Man, I mean I jumped up so fast, I was like airborne. So I go hauling ass off into the bushes . . ."

"No pun intended," Randall said.

"Ha ha. You make another joke about the size of my butt, you're gonna find it sitting on your face."

"Now *that's* scary," Emmit said.

Everybody started laughing.

"Anyway, I ran off into the woods and got lost," Sean said. "I didn't find my way back to campus until the end of PT."

I kept working on the engine, giving instructions to the other guys to do things as I worked.

"You really *do* know something about engines," Farhad said after a while. "I thought you were just BS-ing us."

"This one's old, so it's pretty simple," I said.

"If he knows so much, how come he doesn't have it working yet?" Randall said.

I didn't bother to answer him. I kept working.

After a while, Emmit said, "I'm worried about Mike."

"Yeah," Sean said. "I was in the Silent Room for like three hours and I pretty much freaked out. He's been there for two days straight."

Everybody was quiet for a minute.

"I was in there for a week," I said. "You just have to tough it out."

The guys looked at each other. Emmit shook his head. "Nah, Oz, you were in solitary. The Silent Room's a whole different thing."

"Oh," I said. "Well, what is it?"

There was a long moment where nobody said anything. It was like nobody even wanted to think about it.

"It's more of a chair than a room," Randall said finally.

"The room is soundproofed, I think," Farhad said. "But in the middle of the room there's this big chair. It's made out of really heavy wood with padding over it."

"And straps . . ." Emmit said.

Everybody was quiet again.

"What they do," Sean said, "is they put you in the chair and they strap you in. Waist, shoulder, elbows, wrists, knees. Everything's padded. Even the straps. They don't hurt or anything. It's just, you can't move. I mean not at all . . ."

"Then they put a mouthpiece in your mouth so you can't bite your tongue. . . ."

". . . Then they put this leather hood over your face, buckle it shut. . . ."

Everybody was chiming in now.

". . . it covers your eyes, your ears, your mouth. You can breathe. . . ."

". . . but that's about all you can do."

". . . there's no sound, no feeling, nothing to see, nothing to do. . . ."

We sat there some more.

"Sensory deprivation," I said. "My dad told me about experiments they did with that a long time ago."

"Yeah. After a while you start hallucinating. You start hearing things and tasting things. It's like you're dreaming. . . ."

". . . Except you're awake."

Randall shuddered. "Man, let's talk about something else."

"When I got out," Emmit said, "I didn't even know where I was for a while. I could barely remember my name." He paused. "And I was only in there for a few hours."

"Maybe we could get him out," I said.

"He's in a locked room," Emmit said.

"Only Mrs. Kinnear has the key," Randall added.

"I've got a passkey," I said.

Everybody looked at me. "What do you mean?"

"Camryn slipped me a key."

Randall's jaw opened up a little. "You mean like *hot* Camryn? Babealicious Camryn? Dr. Kinnear's Camryn?"

I shrugged, like it was no big deal. "Yeah."

"She gave you a key? To get into . . ."

"Her house. The administration building. Whatever. She told me she stole it from Mrs. Kinnear. She said it opens everything on the campus."

"You *dog*," Emmit said.

"I was wondering," Farhad said. "You didn't seem all that upset about having to slave away over there."

I couldn't help myself. "It wasn't all slaving, my friends," I said.

"Oh you suck, dude!" Randall said.

"I worship you," Farhad said, bowing down in front of me a couple times.

I worked on the engine for a while. Everybody just sat there looking at me.

"So?" Emmit said finally. "How is she?"

"Can you hand me that half-inch wrench?" I said.

"That's how it's gonna be, huh?" Emmit said. "Okay. Okay."

Everybody laughed some more. I took off one of the valve covers and looked inside. "Oh no," I said.

"What?" Sean said.

I shook my head. "We're screwed," I said.

"What do you mean?"

I slapped my forehead. "How could I have missed that?"

"Missed what?" Randall sounded irritated.

I held up the valve cover. There was a tiny round hole in the metal.

"Bullet hole," I said. I pointed at the wreckage of one of the valves. "Bullet went in, hit the valve spring, totally wrecked the shaft of the valve."

"You can fix it, can't you?" Sean said.

"There's no fixing that," I said. "Not without a machine shop."

I set the ruined valve cover on top of the engine. A terrible silence settled over us. Somewhere out in the swamp a gator roared. Sean shivered.

"Come on, guys," I said. "It's over. Let's go see if we can't get Mike out of the Silent Room for a couple hours."

"But—"

I shook my head. "Forget it, guys. We're not getting off the island on this airboat."

We started walking back, feeling pretty down about the whole thing. "Look," I said as we reached campus, "the FBI's on it. We're going to be okay."

"What! The FBI?"

I explained about the FBI agent friend of Mr. Edson.

"What's wrong with you?" Randall said. "How come you didn't tell us this already? Man, if I'd known the FBI was about to show up here, I'd be in bed instead of dicking around out here in the mud all night."

"I was so busy working on the engine, I just forgot."

We went sneaking across campus, up to the administration building. I slid the key in the lock of the front door. It worked fine, so we walked in. The windows were small and there wasn't much light outside to come in, so the place was very dark.

"Which way?" I whispered.

Emmit pointed to the stairs that went down to the lower floor—a sort of basement area. At the bottom of the stairs we found a long hallway—windowless and dank, with a smell like swamp water had been leaking in for years.

I turned on the flashlight I'd gotten from Dr. Kinnear's tool chest, and we walked to the far end of the hall.

"Try the key," Farhad said, pointing at a blue-painted steel door.

I slid my key into the lock, turned it. It worked. The lock clicked open. We entered the room, closed the door, and flipped on the light.

It was just like they'd described. Except somehow grimmer and more frightening. I'd imagined a bare white room. But this had walls made of rock, and the chair in the middle of the room was crudely built out of large pieces of rough wood with foam padding wrapped around them. It looked like a dungeon with an electric chair in the middle.

Slumped over in the chair was Mike. His head was covered with a black leather hood.

"Hey!" I said. "Mike!"

Emmit and I ran over and unhooked the belts that secured his arms, while Farhad took off the hood and then pulled the mouthpiece from between Mike's lips.

"Mike! Hey! Mike!"

Mike lolled in the chair, staring dully at the floor.

"Are you okay, Mike?"

Mike had always seemed like such a tough, scary guy. But the boy in the padded chair seemed more like a little baby. He didn't move, just looked around a little, blinking, like he was confused. His arms were limp and motionless.

"God!" I said. "What's wrong with him?"

"Two days," Sean said. "He's been in here for two days. That would have been enough to kill me."

"This is not good," Emmit said. "This is really not good."

Randall was standing by the door. "We ought to get out of here," he said nervously.

"For chrissake," Emmit said, "for once in your life could you think about somebody else?" Emmit turned back to me and Sean and Farhad. "Let's get him out of the chair, see if we can make him walk. That'll help him."

We undid his legs, lifted him up. But when we tried to let him stand, his legs gave way. His head seemed too heavy for his neck. A long string of drool hung down from his lip. He made no move to wipe it away.

"We've got to get him out of here," I said.

"If we break him out though," Randall said, "they'll figure out who did it. And then they'll put us all in here."

"He's right," Sean said.

"Let's just walk him around," Emmit said. "Help him get his strength back. Maybe they'll let him go this morning."

We kept trying to walk him around and make him stand up, but Mike was dead weight.

"Talk to us, Mike," Emmit said. "You're gonna be alright. We're gonna take care of you. Come on, Mike. Come on!"

But Mike never said anything, never walked, never even supported his own weight. He didn't even seem to be aware that we were in the room with him.

"You think they drugged him or something?" I said.

"Maybe."

Then the room was silent, no sounds but Mike's feet dragging on the linoleum floor.

Finally Randall said, "I'm going. There's nothing we can do for him."

"Randall—" I said. But he was gone.

"Some friend," Emmit said.

"He's right though," Sean said. "We're still going to have to put him back. And this doesn't seem to be helping. He's just gonna have to tough it out."

I said, "But what if—"

"Don't think about that," Farhad said sharply. "Sometimes there's just no good answer. It's not going to help Mike if the rest of us get caught and stuck in here, too."

After a while Emmit looked at his watch. "We need to hook him back up and go."

"There's got to be something we can do," I said.

But Emmit and Farhad were already putting him back in the seat. We had him all buckled in when—for the first time— Mike said something. I had just put on his hood and was about to zip the zipper that covered his eyes. It was just a whisper.

"What?" I said.

His head rose slightly and his eyes met mine. He whispered again. Still, I couldn't make out what he was saying. I leaned forward.

"Say it again," I said.

"I never signed," he said.

When I straightened up, I could see tears running down his face.

"I never signed," he said again.

"Mike . . ."

"Zip me up," he said. "They can't break me."

But his hand was twitching now and something seemed very wrong with his face.

I put the mouthpiece in his mouth, zipped the zipper down the front of the hood that covered his face.

"Stay strong, Mike," I said.

I thought he nodded. But I couldn't be sure.

Even as tired as I was, once I got back to my bed, I couldn't sleep. I just kept seeing Mike's face, the hollowed-out expression in his eyes, the tears running down the sides of his nose.

Part of me was sad for him. And part of me wanted him in that chair forever. Because I knew that as soon as he signed, I'd be the next one in the Silent Room.

So there we were. No boat, no way off this island. Our only hope was Special Agent Carl Suttles of the FBI. And if he failed us? We were in big, big trouble.

Love,

Oz

twenty-five

Dear Dad,

Today I got up, did PT, ate my cold canned green beans and my biscuit, went to class, then immediately fell asleep while Mr. Akempis read to us in his droning voice out of our twenty-year-old textbook. I think he was reading about the Missouri Compromise. But I don't really remember. Truthfully, today was a blur.

At least until Coach Bell walked into class and woke me up and dragged me outside.

"What?" I said. "I didn't do anything."

Coach Bell didn't say anything. I was scared out of my wits. I felt pretty sure that somehow they had found out about us sneaking in on Mike last night. Did they have cameras or alarms or something? I wasn't sure.

We walked into the administration building and up into the same room where I'd had supper with Mr. Shugrue the other night. But Mr. Shugrue wasn't there. Instead, sitting at the big conference table in the middle of the room was a tall blond guy wearing a blue suit and a white shirt, a red necktie, and dark sunglasses. When I walked in he looked up at Coach Bell and said, "That'll be all, Mr. Bell."

Coach Bell cleared his throat. "School policy, sir," he said. "I need to remain here with the young man."

The man in the suit took off his sunglasses and looked at Coach Bell. He had pale blue eyes. "I'm not asking you to leave, Mr. Bell, I'm telling you."

"Uh, sir, we have a concept called *in loco parentis*, whereby we're supposed to, ah—"

The man in the suit cut him off. "I have a concept whereby I'm gonna charge you with obstructing a federal agent if you don't get your overdeveloped biceps out of this room. We clear, Mr. Bell?"

Coach Bell chewed on his gum real hard, then said, "I'll be outside."

When the door closed, the man in the suit winked at me and grinned. "Sit down, Oz," he said. "That's what they call you, right? Oz?"

"Yes, sir," I said.

The man stood, showed me his badge. "Special Agent Carl Suttles, FBI."

I let out a long breath, then sat down. I felt like every muscle in my body was starting to unclench. "You don't know how glad I am to see you," I said.

"I'll bet," he said. His grin faded. "Well, let's get down to business. I'm out here on a pretense. I told these clowns that I needed to interview you as a possible witness relating to a drug case back in your hometown in Virginia. They don't know why I'm really here."

"Good," I said.

"Yeah. Well, there's some good news and some bad news as far as you're concerned. The good news is that the people that you know as Martin Shugrue and Gwen Kinnear *may*—I repeat *may*—be wanted in connection with a murder out in Idaho. Here's the problem. At this moment, I can't say for sure if they're the same people we think they are. Moreover, they were never formally charged with anything. It's sort of a wanted-for-questioning type situation. We're pretty sure they did some bad things. But we don't absolutely know. That's the good news. The bad news is that, without evidence that they're conspiring to commit some kind of fraud here, there's no immediate way we can do anything to help you."

I rubbed the side of my face. "You can't get me out of here?"

He shook his head. "Not today."

"You can at least tell my mom, though, right?"

"Let's talk about that in a minute. First, could you tell me how you ended up here? I want the whole story, every last detail."

So I told him about how Don Guidry had gotten involved with Mom and how he had framed me so it looked like I was turning into this out-of-control teenager. Then I told him about coming to the Briarwood School, being chased by dogs, being put in solitary confinement, and finally being pressured by Mr. Shugrue to sign a bunch of documents about some trust fund that I'd never heard of before.

When I was done, Agent Suttles blew a long, slow breath out of his mouth, so his cheeks puffed up like a chipmunk's.

"Okay," he said. "Here's the thing. As a law enforcement officer, I can only act on evidence. Without evidence, I'm just a guy with a fancy ID card and a pistol."

"What do you mean?"

"Look, as far as the school goes . . . this solitary confinement thing and the Silent Room and whatnot? First, there's an argument that they aren't crimes at all. But assuming they are, these are probably not federal crimes. They sound like state crimes. State or local police would have jurisdiction. It's just not my jurisdiction."

"You're kidding!"

"Hey, I'm just saying that's what Shugrue and Mrs. Kinnear's lawyers would say. If we went in and tried to arrest them today, they'd make bail next week and probably be out of the country the next day. Do you really want these people punished?"

I nodded.

"Then we need to get evidence of a federal crime. What we call wire fraud—basically stealing money and then moving it around using the Internet or phones or whatever—now *that's* a crime I'm empowered to investigate. If these guys are perpetrating a scheme involving wire fraud, then I can move."

"Look," I said, "I just want to get out of here!"

"Sure. Okay. Sure." He put his hands together like he was praying, then leaned forward. "But you understand that if you leave, we have to tell your mom."

"Well, sure, of course!"

"Here's the thing though. Your stepfather—what's his name?"

"Don Guidry."

"Guidry, right. Don Guidry is obviously in cahoots with Shugrue and Mrs. Kinnear. Whatever money they get from you, he's expecting a cut."

"I hadn't thought of that," I said.

"Well, think about this. If we tell your mom about this, she'll have to tell Guidry something. I mean, she's a mother. She'll flip out, won't she?"

"I guess."

"And so Guidry will find out that she knows something. First thing he'll do, he'll call Shugrue."

"You're saying that if I leave here with you . . ."

"Martin Shugrue and Gwen Kinnear will take whatever they've got—probably all your friends' money—and they'll be in Brazil or someplace by tomorrow afternoon."

"That would suck," I said.

"That *would* suck. Furthermore, at this exact moment I couldn't take you away from here even if I wanted to. It's just not legally possible for me to do that until I notify your mom. I'll have to leave you here, get authorization from my boss, fly up to Virginia, get written authorization from your mother . . ." He spread his hands apart. "It could take me two to three days."

I felt like a deflating balloon. For a second there, I'd thought my problems were over.

"Here's another thing," Agent Suttles added. "It's obvious this Don Guidry guy is involved in this scheme. Think what he might do to your mom when he finds out that his little plan has fallen apart."

I hadn't considered that. I didn't want to get Mom hurt—maybe even killed.

"Well . . . what should I do?" I said.

"Look, you're a minor," Special Agent Suttles said. "I really hate being in a position to use a child as an operative of the FBI. But frankly, I don't know what else to do. . . ."

"An operative? What's that mean?"

"Like an informal agent."

My eyes widened. "You want me to be like a secret agent for the FBI?"

He smiled. "Well, not exactly." He picked up a briefcase off the floor, opened it, took something out, set it on the table. It looked like a tube of lipstick with two wires coming off the end. "You know what this is?"

I shook my head.

"It's called a micro-cam. Sometimes called a lipstick camera. It's a tiny video camera."

"Okay . . ."

"If we could prove that these people were forcing kids to sign away their inheritances, then we could lock these jerks up tomorrow. And keep them locked up."

"You want me to, like, wear a wire?"

He nodded. "Sort of like that. You haven't signed these documents, right?"

"Right."

"So. If we could mount this camera on you and have you sit down with this Shugrue character, get him on film threatening you and misleading you and lying to you, then we've got a case. At that point, I could get a warrant, and *bam* they're in jail for a long, long time."

"Wow!" I said. On the one hand, I wanted to get out of there right this minute. But on the other, I liked the idea of personally sticking it to these jerks. Seeing Mrs. Kinnear led off in handcuffs because of my efforts—that would make up for a whole lot of toilet cleaning.

"Well, here's the thing," I said. "We keep talking about this trust fund. But I don't have a trust fund."

The FBI agent reached into his briefcase, took out a photocopy of a newspaper article. "I did a little research before I came out here," he said, pushing the photocopy across the table to me.

The headline said: AILING INVENTOR WINS CONTRACT. There was a picture of you, Dad, with your name underneath.

"What . . ." I said.

"Six months before your father died, he signed a contract with the General Motors Corporation for them to license a little valve that's used in the fuel injection system of their vehicles. Apparently it's quite revolutionary."

"So?"

"According to the contract, he was to receive about thirty-eight cents every time they used this valve."

"Thirty-eight cents?" I was getting more and more puzzled. "So what? I don't see what—"

"Son, the General Motors Corporation has sold over two million cars every year since your father licensed this technology. The money stopped coming in this year, when a new technology hit the market, but still, you're rich. Your father put all of the money that was going to flow from the contract into a trust fund. For you, Oz. Of course, you're not allowed to touch it until you're twenty-one. I'm sure that's why your mom never told you about it."

"Yeah, but . . . Thirty-eight cents? What's the big deal?"

"That's thirty-eight times, well, six million cars sold in the past three years. That's over two million bucks."

I stared at him.

"Oz, you're a millionaire."

I couldn't believe it. Camryn's stepmom was trying to rip me off for two million dollars? And to top it off she was making me clean out toilets. Talk about adding insult to injury! It made my blood boil.

I picked up the lipstick camera. "What do I need to do, Agent Suttles?" I said.

So maybe things are finally getting better, Dad. Boy, it's about time, huh?

Love,

Oz

twenty-six

Dear Dad,

At supper I was sitting with my roommates when Mike walked into the cafeteria. He moved like an old man, shuffling slowly, a vague expression on his face. Coach Bell carried his tray out for him, set it down for him at a table by himself. The whole cafeteria was silent, staring at him. By now everybody in the school knew how long he'd been in the Silent Room. Supposedly the record up until that point had been like six hours.

Coach Bell glared around the room. "Stop staring!" he shouted. "There's nothing to look at."

Mike, however, didn't seem to notice. He looked at the food for a while, then finally picked up his fork. He looked defeated, wrecked.

"I think he signed," I said.

Farhad shook his head. "I don't even want to think about it."

"He totally signed," Emmit said.

Randall nodded morosely. "Yeah."

I got up and walked over to Mike's table. "Hey," I said. "Why don't you come sit with us?"

He looked up at me, and for a minute it was like he didn't even recognize me. Finally he said, "Go away."

"Look—"

"Get away from me!" he screamed. When he got angry before, he had always seemed scary. But now he just seemed pathetic.

I raised my hands and backed away. "Just asking," I said.

I went back and sat down.

There was a gloomy silence for a while, then Sean started retelling the story of how he'd woken up next to the gator the night before, adding more humorous details. Pretty soon everybody was laughing. I snuck a look over at Mike. He had stopped eating and was just sitting there staring at his food with this blank expression on his face. I sort of tuned Sean out for a minute.

Suddenly something he said caught my attention.

"Wait a minute," I said. "What did you just say, Sean?"

"I was just telling about all these creepy buildings I found back in the woods."

"What creepy buildings?"

"Well, this used to be some kind of research facility owned by the government, right?" he said. "I guess there are more buildings on this island than we knew about."

"You didn't tell me about this earlier."

"I forgot."

"What was in the buildings?"

"All kinds of old machines and stuff. There was this one building that had a sign over the door that said GENERATOR. And another that said MACHINE SHOP."

I stared at him. "There's a machine shop on this island?" I said incredulously. "Does it actually have anything inside?"

Sean shrugged vaguely. "Just a bunch of dusty old machines."

"Sean!" I said. "Why didn't you tell me that earlier?"

"What's the big deal?"

"You ding-a-ling!" I said. Then I dropped my voice to a near whisper. "If there's a machine shop, I could fix the valve on the engine. I might be able to get the boat started."

Sean blinked. "Are you serious?"

"Maybe," I said. "It's worth a try."

Randall groaned. "Dude, I'm sick of staying up all night. I'm waiting on the FBI."

"Look," I said. "It sounds like they're gonna be a while."

"What," Randall said scornfully, "the FBI is gonna let a bunch of kids get whacked? I don't think so!"

"Hey, fine, whatever," I said. "I'll do it myself."

I reached into my pocket, took out a key, slid it across the table to Emmit.

"What's this for?" Emmit said.

"It's the passkey."

"Why are you giving it to me?"

"You'll know when the time comes," I said.

A small furrow formed on his forehead, just above his nose.

I stood up, walked over to Mike's table. Mike was just sitting there, staring. One hand was lying on the table next to his tray, twitching like somebody was running electricity through it.

"Hey!" I yelled. I was staring at the teachers' table. Mr. Akempis, Coach Bell, and the other teachers looked over at me. "Look at this kid!" I pointed at Mike, who just sat there expressionlessly. "You people should be ashamed of yourselves. This is not education. This is not behavior training. This is not helping wayward kids. That's all a big fat lie. And you know it!"

Mr. Akempis's eyes narrowed. He turned and whispered something to Coach Bell.

"You need to chill, Oz," Coach Bell said.

"No!" I shouted. "I'm not gonna chill! This is torture! Look at him. This is good old-fashioned torture. Someday people are going to find themselves in jail because of this."

"Keep your voice down," Mr. Akempis said. He was looking all nervous and weird, little red spots forming on his cheekbones.

I looked around at all the kids. "Torture!" I yelled, thrusting my fist in the air. "Torture! Torture!"

I was kind of curious to see if they'd join in or not.

"Torture! Torture! Torture!"

Nobody said a word. Other than my voice, the room was completely silent. No one moved. No one met my eye.

"Torture! Torture!" I kept punching the air with my fist.

Next thing I knew, Coach Bell had grabbed me in a bear hug and yanked me off my feet.

"Go ahead," I yelled. "Torture me! See if I care!"

Coach Bell hauled me out of the cafeteria and into the quad. Once we got out of the cafeteria, I stopped struggling.

"What in the hell is wrong with you, Oz?" Coach Bell said.

I didn't say anything.

"I'm gonna have to report this to Mrs. Kinnear," he said. "You understand that, don't you?"

"What, and I'm not going to get to see Mom at Parents Day?" I said. "Big deal. You weren't going to let me see her anyway."

Coach Bell just shook his head and marched me across the quad.

Two minutes later I was sitting in the Silent Room, struggling as hard as I could while Mr. Pardee and Coach Bell strapped me into the chair. When they were done with the straps, they left the room. They hadn't put the hood or the mouthpiece in, however. It was already a horrible, claustrophobic feeling. I couldn't imagine how bad it was going to be once the hood and the mouthpiece went on.

"Torture!" I yelled. "Torture!"

I kept yelling until the door opened and Mrs. Kinnear walked in. Then I got quiet.

Mrs. Kinnear crossed the room and stood in front of me. "Oh, this is very sad," she said. "Very distressing. You're just not getting with the program here."

"Whatever," I said.

"You think this is torture? My gracious, you have not learned a single thing here, have you?"

"I've learned you're a sadistic wacko," I said. "But other than that? No, not really."

She smiled coolly. "Sadism has nothing to do with it. Dr. Kinnear conducted a great deal of interesting research into behavior modification. Fifteen years ago he did quite a fascinating study of sensory deprivation. He found it was quite useful for gaining compliance from young people who had difficulty controlling their behavior." She smiled. "Sadly, there were some negative side effects and he had to abandon the research."

I met her gaze, stared defiantly back at her. I didn't really feel all that defiant. But I figured I'd come this far, I better not back down.

"Dr. Kinnear found that the negative side effects started kicking in after three hours in the Silent Room. Six hours produced quite serious problems. Only one person was experimented on for more than twenty hours. It took him several months to recover." She cocked her head. "Say, would you like to sign those, ah, admission forms? If you did that, I could see my way clear to putting you into solitary confinement instead of leaving you here in the Silent Room."

"In your dreams," I said. "I'm not signing away my trust fund."

One carefully plucked eyebrow went up slightly. "My, my. We really are just too clever for our own good, aren't we?"

"I think that's your department."

"Alrighty then," she said cheerfully. "Let's see how that attitude works for you after twenty-four hours in this chair."

I smiled at her.

She picked up a red mouthpiece that was attached to one arm of the chair by a piece of dirty string. "Open wide," she said.

I didn't move.

"Hey, I could have Mr. Pardee come in here and knock your teeth out with a hammer," she said.

I opened my mouth.

She put the mouthpiece in. It was gritty and tasted disgusting. Next thing I knew, she had the hood on my head. She grabbed the zipper with her red-nailed fingers.

"Sweet dreams," she said.

ZIPPPP. And the world was gone. No sound, no light, no sensation, no nothing.

I had this sinking feeling that I'd just made a seriously big mistake.

Sensory deprivation is one of those things that you have to experience to understand. You can't explain just how horrible it is. I mean, it sounds like nothing. And at first—yeah—it's no big deal. Mostly just irritating. You keep getting itchy. And of course you can't scratch. Pretty soon all you can think about is itching. My back felt like it was crawling with bugs or something. I mean, I knew there weren't any bugs there . . . but still. It *seemed* like they were there.

Then things get worse.

But let me back up . . . You might be curious why I'd gotten myself stuck there in the Silent Room.

Simple. Because I had to do it this way. I had discussed it with Special Agent Suttles and he had said that if I just went into Mrs. Kinnear's office and volunteered to sign, she'd be suspicious. But if I let them punish me a little bit and *then* agreed to sign so they wouldn't punish me anymore, it would seem more believable. It had seemed like a good idea back when I was sitting in the room with the FBI agent. There'd even been something kind of fun about screaming at the teachers in the cafeteria while all the kids watched.

But now? With the make-believe bugs crawling all over my back? It seemed like a much dumber idea.

Fortunately, after a while the itching stopped. At that point my mind just started wandering. I kept imagining that I was hearing things. Little clicks and pops. Like the door was opening. Only, it wasn't. I kept thinking, *How long have I been here?* Had it been a minute? Five? Ten? An hour? A century? I had no way of telling.

For a while I think I slept. I wasn't really sure. It was hard to tell when I was sleeping or dreaming or hallucinating. At one point I imagined that my hood had come off. I felt like I was just sitting in the Silent Room, looking around. For a minute I was convinced that it was really happening, that somebody had come in while I had nodded off and taken off my hood. But then when dead soldiers started walking out of the walls, I realized, okay maybe not. They were all wearing military coveralls and they all had been shot. Some of them in the chest, some in the face, some in the neck. Bleeding all over. They never talked; they just looked at me. Then they'd walk over and stand by me and their blood would drip off. I could feel it going drip, drip, drip, drip on my arms.

I tried to tell them to go away, but they just stood there staring.

I mean, part of me knew it was a hallucination. But part of me was convinced it was real. Then I was just sort of drifting again in the dark, seeing lights that went on and off and hearing sounds. Clicks, pops, car horns, sirens, birds—just random sounds. But they all seemed creepy and menacing. I imagined people were sneaking into the room and walking around me with nail clippers and knives and can openers and stuff. I could feel them cutting bits of skin off my legs or pressing their blades down deep in my flesh. Or sometimes I imagined that birds were about to land on my face and tear my eyes out.

And then after a while things got really vague and I felt like I was floating in a black lake of oil and dark, evil things were moving slowly around me, watching and waiting.

I do not like this. I do not like this at all.

Love,

Oz

twenty-seven

Dear Dad,

I lost track of time. But suddenly someone was taking my hood off. For a second I thought it was you, Dad. But then I saw that it was Emmit.

"You okay, Oz?" he said.

I tried to say something, but it was like my tongue was made of wood. It felt like one of those wooden clackers we used in music class when I was in kindergarten. For some reason this seemed really funny.

"Clacker," I said.

"What?" Emmit frowned, leaned toward me.

"Clacker," I said. "Clacker, clacker, clacker."

"I think he's saying 'cracker.'" It was Sean's voice behind me.

"We don't have crackers," Emmit said. "You want a biscuit?"

"Clacker. Clacker. Clacker. Clacker." I started laughing. Except the laugh came out all goony and retarded-sounding.

"I think he's a little messed up," Farhad said.

"Just get him unhitched," Emmit said.

Eventually they got me disconnected from the chair. "What time is it?" I said.

"Midnight. You were in the Silent Room for five hours," Sean said.

"Man," I said. "No wonder Mike turned into a halfway vegetable. Five hours seems like forever."

"Can you walk?" Emmit said.

"Oh, sure," I said. But when I tried to stand up, my legs gave out and I fell over. It was weird. I didn't feel weak or anything, but it was like my body had forgotten how to move.

They stood me up again and this time I was able to kind of shuffle around.

"Let's go," I said.

By the time I got to the airboat, I was feeling pretty good. A little slow, a little dopey. But basically okay.

"So where's this machine shop?" I said to Sean.

"Uh . . ." he said. "I'm not sure."

"Oh, you're kidding me!" Farhad said.

"Hey, you try paying attention when you're running away from a thirty-foot-long alligator."

"You sure it wasn't sixty feet?" Farhad said.

"Ha ha," Sean said. "Hey, it was *big*. That's all I know."

"Look, the building's got to be close," I said. "Right?"

"There must have been paths or roads back when the army ran this whole place," Emmit said. "If we start working our way through the woods, we'll find one. Then we just follow it wherever it leads. Easy."

It sounded easy. But it turned out not to be. We spent about three hours tromping around in the woods. But finally we did find it. Two buildings—both of them lightless and creepy-looking. Sean shined his flashlight around until we saw the sign over the front door of one of them: MACHINE SHOP.

"Let's go see," I said.

We walked to the door, tried the handle. It was padlocked shut with an ancient, rusted chain. On the door was an ancient sign that said: U.S. GOVERNMENT PROPERTY. TRESPASSERS SUBJECT TO CRIMINAL PROSECUTION.

"Prosecute this," Farhad said. Then he kicked the window next to the door. It shattered with an enormous noise.

"I hope nobody heard that back at the school," Sean said.

Immediately we heard another noise, though. Mr. Pardee's dogs started howling and snarling. They were a long way away. But still, we could hear them.

"Oh, crap," Emmit said. "They'll wake everybody."

But after a minute the dogs quieted down. We climbed through the window and went inside.

As Sean had told us, there were all kinds of huge machines scattered around the room. I took his flashlight, surveyed the room. End mills, drill presses, lathes—it was a machinist's paradise. Dad, it was just like the equipment you used in your shop. These machines were all really old—probably going back to World War II. But they all looked like high-quality tools.

"Cool!" Emmit said.

"Now all we need is power," I said. "Somebody try a light switch."

Farhad walked to the front door, flipped a switch on the wall. Nothing.

"There should be a main fuse box where the power comes in," I said. "It could be that it's just turned off."

"What's that?" Emmit pointed his flashlight at a large gray metal box on the wall.

"That's it." I walked over, popped open the door to the box, looked inside. There was a big switch handle like Dr. Frankenstein always throws in the movies when he's about to make the monster come alive. It was set to the *off* position. I grabbed the handle, yanked on it until it moved down to the *on* position.

"Try the lights again," I said.

Farhad went around flipping various switches. But nothing came on.

"Hm . . ." I said.

"So what do we do now?" Emmit said.

"Wait a minute," Farhad said. "The building next door says GENERATOR on the door."

"Let's check it out," I said.

We climbed back out the broken window and walked to the other building.

We had to break out another window to get in. But sure enough, in the back of the building was a gas-powered electrical power generator in a small room. I went inside, turned on the motor, hit the "start" switch. As I expected, nothing happened. There was a gas tank next to the engine. I opened the fill knob, sniffed. There was still gas inside. It was probably a million years old. But as far as I knew, gas didn't go bad.

"Battery's dead," I said.

"Can we use the golf-cart battery?"

I nodded.

"I'll go get it," Farhad said.

He and Sean left together. It took them about fifteen minutes to get back with the battery. I hooked it up, hit the *start* button.

The engine coughed and spluttered and a bunch of black smoke belched out the little exhaust stack. The lights flickered on in the room.

"Yes!" I said.

Then, suddenly, an incredibly loud wailing sound began to rise around us. It grew louder and louder, higher and higher in pitch. I hit the *off* button. The engine died, the lights went out, and the awful shrieking noise wound down into silence.

"What in the world was that?" Emmit said.

"It sounded like one of those air-raid sirens they used back in World War II," I said.

"Maybe they left it on intentionally when they closed this place down," Emmit said. "As a sort of makeshift alarm."

"You think they heard it back at the school?" I said.

"Of course they did," Emmit said. "I mean, unless everybody in the whole school suddenly went stone deaf."

"Shh!" Sean said.

We all got quiet.

Then we heard it. The dogs again. We waited, hoping they'd quiet down again, like they did when we broke the window. But this time they didn't. Instead of quieting down, they just kept barking.

"What are we gonna do?" Sean said.

"We better run," I said. "Before Mr. Pardee gets out there and sets them on us."

We raced back to the administration building and hid out for a while. We could hear people outside moving around, and the dogs were barking and running all over. Eventually though, the dogs stopped barking and apparently everybody went back to sleep.

"Well?" Emmit said to me.

I didn't say anything, just started walking down into the basement, pulled open the door of the Silent Room. The musty stink of the place made me feel queasy.

I took a deep breath, walked over to the chair, sat down, pulled the hood over my face. I felt like tendrils of darkness were snaking out, pulling at my mind, ready to drag me off into someplace where Oswald Turner was only a fading memory, sinking into a black empty void. *It's just my imagination,* I told myself. *It's nothing. I can take it.*

"Okay," I said. "Let's do it."

Love,

Oz

twenty-eight

Dear Dad,

So I guess I spent the rest of the night and most of the day in the Silent Room. I tried to concentrate on specific thoughts and not let my mind wander. I thought about how I would fix the engine, trying to figure out how I would use the lathe to make a new valve. But I kept running into problems in my mind, problems I didn't know how to solve. And eventually I just ran out of steam. After that, I thought about Camryn, what it felt like kissing her. Then after a while, I thought about how good it would feel to watch Mrs. Kinnear get hauled off in handcuffs.

So far everything was fine. I had the Silent Room under control. No hallucinations, no crazy thoughts, no dead guys walking through the walls.

At some point I fell asleep.

It was when I woke up that the problems started.

The first thing was terror. When I woke up, I didn't know where I was. All I knew was that I couldn't move, couldn't see, couldn't hear, couldn't feel anything. I was totally disoriented.

Eventually I remembered where I was. Then I started getting this panicky feeling, like I couldn't breathe. I started thrashing around and stuff. But it didn't do any good. They had snugged me in nice and tight. After a while I just got worn-out.

And then I was drifting again in the lake of oil, just like I had done earlier in the night. I may have had some hallucinations, but I don't really remember most of them. I do remember thinking I was at home in bed for a minute. I could hear Mom downstairs making something in the kitchen. Then I smelled cookies. But it wasn't exactly like I was there. There were some other hallucinations. Nothing dramatic or weird. Just normal stuff, like being in school and eating fish sticks in the cafeteria. Or running through this field with you, Dad, flying a kite.

But each hallucination felt more and more vague and distant. I felt like I was getting farther and farther from my life. Like I was floating around in space, and the kid I used to be was down there in the chair, and we were not the same person anymore. I imagined that I was attached to the boy in the chair by a rubber band. And the farther I drifted away, the tighter the rubber band got. Eventually I knew that the rubber band would snap. And when it did, I would be separated forever from the boy in the chair.

And that would be the end of him.

Toward the end I had the strangest sensation. It was like you were there with me, Dad. I could hear your voice. You were saying, "Come on with me, Oz. Leave that boy in the chair. He's just a dirty bag of flesh. He's weak. He's pathetic. Come with me. Come with me, Oz."

And I wanted to. I wanted to be with you again. For a minute I remembered being eight or ten years old back on the farm. And I was out in your machine shop, watching you work. I was sitting on top of a box, swinging my legs. And you were using the lathe, cutting something out of a steel rod.

A valve. You were cutting a valve, and telling me how to do it. Everything I needed to know—how to cut the shoulder, how to relieve the edges, how to narrow down the neck without breaking the tool. . . . And then I was drifting again.

You smiled at me, Dad. The valve was between your fingers. Then you threw it real softly and it went off into the blackness and disappeared and you said, "You don't need this anymore. Just come with me and leave that dirty boy behind."

I could feel the rubber band stretching and stretching, just about to break. And for a minute, Dad, I almost went. I wondered: is this what it feels like to die?

After that I don't remember anything.

And then, suddenly, there was light. It felt like it was burning right through my head, like when you look into the bright fire of a welding torch. Except instead of a single point of light, the whole world had gone blindingly bright. Then I could see dark fuzzy things moving in the light.

"Well, well," a voice said. "Someone's looking awfully compliant this afternoon."

It took me a while, but then I recognized it as Mrs. Kinnear. I don't know why, but I felt really happy to see her. I felt this big wave of gratitude and relief, like I used to feel when I was a little kid getting home from first grade and seeing Mom. I felt like, *Okay, now somebody's going to take care of me.* I mean in the back of my mind I knew it was crazy. But that part of my brain felt like it was buried in sludge.

Mrs. Kinnear had a towel in her hands. She wiped my face with the towel and then combed my hair back with her fingers. I felt happy. I wanted to make her feel happy. I wanted her to like me.

"Can he walk?" she said.

I wanted to walk. I tried to. But nothing really moved.

"Pick him up, would you?" she said to somebody. I couldn't see his face, but I was sure it was Coach Bell. Mr. Pardee must have been with him, because I felt two people lifting me up and carrying me.

We went out of the room, down the hall, up two flights of stairs, and into the conference room. Mr. Shugrue was sitting at the table with a bunch of papers in front of him.

"Here's our boy!" he said in this real cheery way. "How you doing, pal?"

"Fine!" I said. Except it came out more like, *Funnhhhg.*

I was happy to see Mr. Shugrue.

"You ready to sign some papers?"

I blinked. Sure. I was ready to do anything for Mr. Shugrue. Mr. Shugrue and Mrs. Kinnear had taken me out of the Silent Room. Anybody who would do that for somebody . . .

I opened my mouth and closed it a couple times. There was something I needed to do. But what was it?

"He's been in for twelve hours," Mrs. Kinnear said. "It's going to take him a little while before he's able to sign."

"Oh, for godsake," Mr. Shugrue said, suddenly irritated. "I thought you said he'd do anything you told him."

"This is not a predictable thing," Mrs. Kinnear said. "Everybody reacts differently."

"So I'm just supposed to sit here twiddling my thumbs for an hour?"

Mrs. Kinnear gave him a withering look. "What? Two million dollars is not worth an hour of thumb twiddling?"

Mr. Shugrue gave her his cheesy smile. "You make a good point, Gwen," he said.

And all the time they were talking, I kept thinking: *There's something I'm supposed to do. What is it I'm supposed to do?*

Then, finally, I remembered. The lipstick camera. It was hidden under my arm, taped there with duct tape. There was a tiny hole that I'd cut into my shirt. I needed to adjust the fabric so that the camera would be able to aim out through the hole.

Why was this so important? I really couldn't remember.

And besides, I could barely move.

I thought about it for a while. Agent Suttles and I had worked out a system. I would pretend to scratch my underarm. And as I was "scratching," I would adjust my T-shirt.

Then I had to turn on a recorder that was taped to my back. We were too far from anywhere to use a transmitter, Agent Suttles had told me. So I had to record the video to a small digital device, sort of like an iPod, but for video.

All of this went running through my mind, but for a minute I couldn't make any sense of it. It just didn't seem urgent.

I sat there for a while and then suddenly I reached up and scratched myself.

"Did you see that?" Mr. Shugrue said.

"What?"

He was pointing at my arm, right where the camera was.

For a minute I thought he'd seen the camera. But then all he said was, "He just scratched himself."

"So?"

"If he can scratch himself, maybe he can sign."

"Ask him," Mrs. Kinnear said.

"You ready to sign, bud?" Mr. Shugrue said to me.

"What am I signing?" I said. Suddenly I could talk.

"Just some admission forms."

"Bull," I said.

"Hey!" Mr. Shugrue said, turning to Mrs. Kinnear. "Look, he's staged a remarkable recovery. He's turned back into a little smart-ass again."

"You want to go back into the Silent Room?" Mrs. Kinnear said to me.

"No."

"Then shut up and sign the papers."

My emotions were flip-flopping. Now I didn't feel any affection for her at all. I was just really afraid of her. I didn't want to go back in the Silent Room. "Please, no," I said.

"Sign the papers and you can go back to class. Everything will be normal again."

I remembered vaguely that Agent Suttles had stressed one thing to me: I had to make them admit to what I was signing, that they knew these weren't just admission forms. "Tell me what the papers say." My tongue felt thick.

"I don't see any reason for that," Mr. Shugrue said. "Just sign them."

I sat there in silence for a minute. "Then, no," I said.

Mr. Shugrue looked at Mrs. Kinnear. She shrugged. "If it'll get him to sign . . ."

"Okay," Mr. Shugrue said. "Look, here's the deal. Your father established a trust fund for you before he died. A trust is a legal entity that is administered by a lawyer who is named in the trust incorporation documents. Even if you wanted to take money from the trust, you can't. Not until you're twenty-one."

"Then what good is it going to do to have me sign anything?" I said.

"What you'll sign is a document that allows for the transferal of administration of the trust. Your mom has to consent to this and so do you. Your stepfather has already convinced her to sign. So it's all on you now. You sign and a new trust administrator will be named."

"And who will that be?"

He shoved a document in front of my face. "That would be Martin R. Shugrue, attorney at law."

"So once you get your hands on the money . . ."

He smiled. "Hey, it wasn't really your money anyway. So don't worry about it. You're a bright young kid. You got your whole life ahead of you. You'll do great."

I put my hand up to where the camera was, making sure the lens was still poking through the shirt. It was. I felt pretty good. Agent Suttles was going to be proud of me. Mr. Shugrue was sitting there all smug and jolly. I felt like saying, "Dude, you've been punked!" or something. But I didn't.

"Shut up, Martin," Mrs. Kinnear said. Then she turned to me. "Quit stalling. Sign the forms."

I sort of hesitated.

"Coach Bell, would you take Oswald back to the Silent Room?"

I felt a wave of terror, just at the sound of it.

"Okay! Okay!" I said. "I'm signing." I didn't have to fake my fear. I really, really didn't want to go back in that room.

Mr. Shugrue pointed out the various places that I had to sign. Then when I was all done he said, "Good man! We're all set."

"Can I go now?" I said.

"Well, there's one last thing," Mr. Shugrue said.

As he spoke, the door opened and a man walked in. It was Agent Suttles.

"Thank God you're here!" I said.

But then I felt this sense of confusion. There was something different about Agent Suttles. No suit, for one thing. He was wearing tight blue jeans, cowboy boots with very pointy toes, and a black T-shirt with a picture of that country singer Kenny Chesney on it. I can't tell you how much I hate Kenny Chesney. Also he was wearing lots of tacky gold bling. But it wasn't really that. It was more that his expression had changed. There was something cold there, something I hadn't seen in his eyes before.

Agent Suttles reached out toward me, lifted up my T-shirt, and yanked out the video camera. The duct tape felt like it ripped out about half my underarm hair.

"Ow!" I said.

He tossed the video camera on the table in front of Mr. Shugrue.

"Nice work, Leon," Mr. Shugrue said. "I mean . . . *Agent Suttles.*"

Then everybody in the room started laughing.

I felt a cold sensation running down my spine. They'd played me like a violin.

"But how . . ." I said. Somebody had ratted me out. Who was it? Randall? Sean? Who?

Agent Suttles looked at me with his cold blue eyes, then raised one eyebrow slightly.

"But I thought . . ."

"You thought I wouldn't find out that you were using Camryn's computer to run searches on us?" Mrs. Kinnear said. "You thought somebody wouldn't see you and that moron Edson whispering behind that bush? You thought I would just let an FBI agent wander onto school property and talk to anybody he pleased? You really are naive."

"What happened to Mr. Edson?" I said.

"Let's just say he didn't get a chance to cash that check we gave him," Mr. Shugrue said.

For a minute I felt like I might throw up.

"Take him back to the Silent Room," Mrs. Kinnear said.

"Why!" I said. "I signed! I did everything you wanted!"

"Leon?" Mrs. Kinnear said to the guy who had claimed to be Agent Suttles. "Take him now. His voice is really starting to grate on me."

"But why?" I screamed.

Mrs. Kinnear reached out, stroked the side of my face with one long red fingernail, then smiled brightly. "Because I don't like you, Oswald," she said.

> Your son,
>
> Oz

twenty-nine

Dear Dad,

Thank goodness, they came and got me again around midnight. If I'd stayed there till morning, there's no telling what would have happened. Even when they did, I couldn't walk and for a while I wasn't even sure who they were. I remember dark figures carrying me on their backs. I remember flashlights moving around in the dark. My mind was still halfway back in the Silent Room for a good while. I kept thinking that I was dreaming or hallucinating. And some of the time, I think I was.

Later they told me that I just sat there for over an hour and they couldn't get me to do anything. But then suddenly I just stood up.

I don't really remember. The first thing I recall was standing there staring at the boat. And in my mind I had this overpowering thought:

One more night.

This was it. One night to get the engine fixed and get out of this place. If we didn't, there was a good chance that some of us would wind up dead. Back in Idaho, Mrs. Kinnear and Martin Shugrue had proved that they would kill anybody who stood between them and the money.

To tell the truth? I didn't really see any way of fixing the engine in one night. But I had to try.

I started fumbling around, removing the broken valve. My fingers felt like wood and my mind kept drifting off into the darkness. But something in the back of my mind just kept pushing me to keep going, keep going.

"If we're going to use that lathe," I said, "I'm going to need power from the generator. And to get power, we're going to have to find out where that siren is and disconnect it."

"I'll go over there and start searching," Emmit said.

The more I thought about it, the more it seemed like this was not a doable project. Even if there was a piece of steel the right size for me to machine, it would take a very long time to machine it. And if I got all the measurements exactly right— and my guess was that I wouldn't—then I'd still have to put the engine back together properly and get it running without new gaskets and without any guarantee that there weren't other problems that had yet to be fixed. Which I might or might not be able to figure out. And which I might or might not have the parts to fix, even if I knew what needed to be done.

It took me about half an hour, but I finally got the valve removed.

"Where's Emmit?" I said.

Sean shrugged. I had been concentrating on the engine so much that I wasn't thinking about anything else. Suddenly I felt worried. "He should be done by now. We better go find him."

We hiked over to the machine shop, looked around for Emmit.

"Emmit!" Sean called softly.

No answer.

I didn't like it.

"Maybe he got lost," I said.

"Maybe he's inside one of the buildings and can't hear us."

We stood there for a minute, waving our flashlights around, hoping to catch a glimpse of him.

Suddenly I heard something. "What's that?" Sean said.

I held my finger up to my lips.

After a moment, I heard it again. A very low growl. I felt the hair rise on my neck.

"What is that?" Sean said. "A gator?"

I shook my head. "Dogs," I whispered. "It's a trap."

Sean's shoulders sagged. "Mr. Pardee or Coach Bell must be waiting for us inside the building. He's probably already got Emmit."

I nodded.

"What are we gonna do?"

I pointed at the building where the generator was located. "You go over there to the generator building. Go back to the generator room and open the door."

"And then what?"

"Wait."

Sean didn't move.

"Now," I said. "Go."

Sean started walking toward the building. I could feel Mr. Pardee's eyes on me. I didn't know where he was, but I was sure he must be watching us.

I waited until Sean disappeared, then I started walking toward the machine shop. My heart was beating fast. Half of me just wanted to go running back into the woods. But by now there was no turning back. If Mr. Pardee was there, he knew I was supposed to be in the Silent Room. Which meant he also wouldn't let me get away, no matter what.

I paused at the door of the machine shop. I heard something inside. A soft clicking. The sound of dog claws on linoleum.

Well, I thought. *Here goes nothing.*

I opened the door. The dogs burst out and I started running for the building where the generator was located.

The dogs were right behind me. I had almost made it to the door of the generator building when the first dog sank its teeth into the cuff of my blue jeans. I tripped and hit the ground. The dog lost its grip on my pants as I spun head over heels. By total luck, my foot kicked the dog and it went flying, too.

I rolled, came to my feet just as one of the other dogs pounced. I sidestepped, the Doberman's long teeth barely missing my arm as it barreled by, knocking the third dog out of my way. I accelerated through the door and into the main room of the generator building, started running down the bare, lightless hallway.

I could hear the clicking of claws and the growls of the

dogs behind me. It was about twenty yards to the end of the hallway. The dogs were sliding around on the slippery floor.

"Open the door, Sean!" I yelled. "Open the door!"

I was getting closer and closer, and the door wasn't opening.

"Now, Sean! The door!"

The dogs were getting nearer with every step I took.

Just as I'd about given up hope, the door opened. I charged through and Sean slammed the door shut.

The Dobermans were barking and growling, their bodies hammering against the door.

"What now?" Sean said. His face was pale and he was sweating.

"We've got to get around to the front door and lock it up before the dogs figure out we've gotten outside."

He swallowed. "Uh. How about I stay here and distract them? You go around and get the door."

I nodded, yanked open the back door of the generator room and sprinted around the side of the building toward the front door. I could hear the dogs inside, still growling and barking.

I reached the front door, slammed it shut. *Okay,* I thought. *One problem down.* Now all I had to do was take care of Mr. Pardee.

I heard something behind me, a soft crunching noise. I whirled around.

"Good thinking, boy." It was Mr. Pardee. "Take the dogs out of the equation, now you got nothing to worry about but an old man."

I couldn't really see his face. But I could make out his pale blue eyes, glowing in a reflected shaft of moonlight.

"Problem is," Mr. Pardee said, "I thought of that myself." He gave a low whistle. The fourth dog trotted out of the machine shop. "So I kept one of the dogs in reserve. Just in case."

He moved slightly, coming into the moonlight. I could see a smile on his face. The dog stood next to him, panting slightly, its eyes never leaving me.

"What you gonna do now, boy?" Mr. Pardee said.

"Run?" I said.

"Won't do you no good." He chuckled. "But then again I reckon it's your best shot, huh?"

I didn't move.

"What." His voice was scornful. "You just gonna give up, boy?"

Alright, I thought. It was me against one dog.

"I'll give you a ten-second head start," the old man said, "just to make it sporting." He laughed harshly.

I started running.

"One, two . . ." I could hear the old man counting. ". . . three, four . . . go!" The old man laughed again. So I guess he didn't want it *that* sporting.

I made it into the trees and started heading for the water. I didn't really have any strategy. I just figured maybe I could lose the dog by swimming out into the lake or something.

The dog didn't bark, didn't growl—it just tore after me, a black streak through the trees. Let me tell you something: a four-second head start isn't much when it comes to racing a Doberman pinscher.

I clambered over fallen trees and splashed through shallow ponds and then suddenly I was at the airboat. The dog burst out of the trees and came up short just in front of me. It was about five feet from me, growling softly. I backed toward the airboat. The dog followed. I tried to dodge sideways, but the dog cut me off, baring its teeth. I stepped back. It stepped forward.

It was obvious what the dog was doing: as long as it had me cornered, it didn't see the need to attack me. But I knew that if I started to run, it was going to start chomping on me.

I backed up another step. Then another. Then another.

On the fourth step, my foot hit a large fallen tree and I fell over backward. This time the dog didn't budge. It just stood there, quivering slightly, teeth bared, growling.

For a moment, nothing moved. And then something unexpected happened.

The log I'd just tripped over moved. Not slowly, like a log rolling over when you step on it. It was fast.

And it wasn't until I saw the jaws open and then clamp down on the Doberman's neck that I realized it wasn't a log at all. The fallen tree was actually an alligator.

It must have been the same gator that had scared Sean off the other day. We'd all been ribbing him, telling him he'd exaggerated the size of the thing. But he hadn't. This one was a monster—big enough to snap a Doberman's neck in two. I remembered what Mr. Edson had said about that hunter killing a thousand-pound gator a few years back. Was this one that big? I don't know. But it was big enough that I didn't feel like sticking around to take measurements.

The dog twitched once or twice, then went limp. The big gator lumbered down to the waterline, slid into the oily blackness, and disappeared.

I backed away from the water. I couldn't believe what had just happened. It had all been over in just a second or two.

I looked up and there was Mr. Pardee. "My goodness," he said. "If that ain't the most beautiful thing I ever seen . . ."

"Beautiful?" I said. "That thing ate your dog and you call it beautiful?"

"My *best* dog, too," the old man said. He smiled. "But, hey— it don't pay to get attached to no animal." His shoulders went up and down a couple times like he was laughing, but he didn't make any sound. "People neither, for that matter."

We looked at each other for a minute. I was trying to think what to do next.

"Don't be trying nothing cute, son," he said.

I heard a splash behind me. I looked around and I saw the huge gator surfacing in the water. The dog was gone. The gator's eyes floated just above the surface of the water, then its tail wagged lazily, drawing a glistening S-shape in the black water. It was probably about thirty yards away from me.

When I turned back around, Mr. Pardee had a pistol in his hand.

"You think he's still hungry?" he said.

I started edging away from the water.

"Nah, nah, nah," the old man said, waggling his pistol. "You just stay right where you are."

I stopped moving, looked over my shoulder. The huge alligator didn't seem to be swimming, but it had gotten closer. Like it was drifting with the current.

There was a soft wind. Everything seemed to be moving very slowly now—the leaves stirring softly in the trees, the old man taking a slow step toward me, the alligator drifting and drifting.

That was when the old man suddenly noticed the airboat. I guess it was so dark that he hadn't been able to make it out before. His eyebrows rose.

"Dadgum! Lookie here! Y'all fixing to escape, ain't you?" he said. He seemed amused.

I didn't say anything. I kept checking nervously over my shoulder. The gator was a couple yards closer.

Mr. Pardee walked slowly to the airboat. He picked up the valve cover, examined it, tossed it back down. It clattered loudly on the aluminum decking of the airboat. "So that's why y'all was at the machine shop, huh? Trying to make you some parts to get this old engine going?"

I didn't say anything. The big gator was about fifteen yards away now. Fifteen yards was way too close.

"Y'all some slippery little bastards, I tell you what."

Slippery. Suddenly an idea struck me.

I shoved my end of the airboat sideways. Because it was sitting on slippery mud, it moved a little. Not much, but a little, swiveling in the center so that as my end of the boat went away from me, the other end pivoted around toward Mr. Pardee. It caught him in the leg and he lost his balance. As he struggled to catch himself, he slipped on the mud and fell down hard. His pistol skittered away from him. I dove for the pistol, grabbed it before Mr. Pardee could reach it.

Looking over at the water, I saw the huge alligator had almost reached land. I scrambled up the bank. Behind me I could hear Mr. Pardee scrambling, too. But the mud was so slick that he was having trouble getting to his feet.

The big alligator was on the land now, lumbering toward Mr. Pardee, its long tail switching back and forth, leaving a snakelike trail in the mud.

"Help me!" the old man said. "For godsake, boy, don't let it get me!"

Why I didn't let the gator eat him, I don't know. I guess I couldn't help thinking that it would be wrong. So I aimed the pistol, fired at the gator. Maybe I missed or something, but it just kept coming toward Mr. Pardee. I fired again, three more times. Suddenly the gator stopped, looked at me, then looked at Mr. Pardee. Its mouth opened wide, like it was yawning. Its jaws were so big, that one of Mr. Pardee's entire legs could have fit inside. It couldn't have been more than eight inches from Mr. Pardee's face. Mr. Pardee froze, his eyes wide.

Suddenly, the gator turned, its big tail whipping around. And inside a second it was back in the water and gone.

I didn't see exactly what happened, but the big tail must have hit the old man's leg, because he was holding his ankle and going, "Oh, my leg! Oh, my leg!"

"Get up," I said.

"I think it broke my leg with its tail," Mr. Pardee whined.

"And I'm supposed to care about that?" I said.

The old man stared at me a minute and then laughed his noiseless laugh. "You got a point," he said. Then he staggered to his feet and started hobbling up the bank.

"Back to the machine shop," I said.

At that moment I heard a beeping noise. A tiny light on the old man's belt started flashing. It was a walkie-talkie.

Then a woman's voice came out of the walkie-talkie. "What's going on, Mr. Pardee? I heard gunshots."

Mr. Pardee looked at me.

"Tell them it's nothing, Mr. Pardee. Tell them you had to shoot an alligator."

Mr. Pardee didn't move.

"Hey," I said. "I've been nice so far. But this time you better do what I tell you." I pointed the gun at his chest.

Mr. Pardee took the radio off his belt, put it to his mouth. "It was just a gator, Mrs. Kinnear," he said.

"I don't pay you to hunt alligators," she said.

"Say, 'Yes, ma'am,'" I said.

"Yes, ma'am," Mr. Pardee said into the radio.

"Did you find any of our clever little scholars playing in the woods again?" Mrs. Kinnear's voice crackled.

"Tell her, 'No, ma'am, I believe they learned their lesson,'" I said.

Mr. Pardee said it just like I told him to.

"Now throw me the radio," I said.

He did as he was told. I pointed with the gun toward the trail. He hobbled forward. Pretty soon we were at the machine shop. The dogs in the other building had calmed down. We went around back, and Sean came out the door of the generator room. His eyes widened when he saw me pointing the gun at Mr. Pardee.

"Oz!" he said. "You rock! What happened?"

"I'll tell you later," I said. Then to Mr. Pardee: "Where's Emmit?"

"Who? That colored boy?"

"The black guy, yeah."

"I duct-taped him to a post inside the machine shop."

"Let's go," I said.

We went inside and found Emmit. Emmit seemed to take a great deal of pleasure in taping Mr. Pardee to the same concrete pillar where the old man had taped him.

Just as we were about to tape Mr. Pardee's mouth up, the leathery old man said, "Y'all ain't gonna make it. It's all gonna be over tomorrow. If I don't show up in the morning, Coach Bell's gonna come out here with a shotgun and take care of you."

"We'll see," I said.

Mr. Pardee laughed harshly. "It's already two thirty in the morning. Y'all ain't gonna be able to fix that engine. Not before sunrise."

"Tape his mouth up, Emmit," I said.

"Plus which, you can't use no tools without firing up the generator. When that engine gets going, it'll set off the sireen, just like it done the other day."

I felt a sinking sensation in my chest. I knew the old man was right. But then suddenly something hit me.

"Who says we need to fix the engine?"

"What do you mean?" Emmit said as he wrapped a loop of tape around Mr. Pardee's face, covering his mouth.

"The generator," I said. "What if we just took the generator motor out and attached it to the airboat?"

Emmit frowned. "You think we could do that?"

"That generator motor is a small block Ford V-8. Same as the one that's in the airboat. If we could get the motor mounts to line up . . ."

Sean and Emmit looked at each other and shrugged.

And that's how easy it was, Dad. We found this little cart on the other side of the machine shop, went back and unbolted the motor from the generator, and hauled it back down to the airboat. The whole setup was simple. All I had to do was punch a couple holes in the mounting blocks and hoist the generator engine onto the boat. It took a little bit of struggle to get the propeller off, but it mounted with a bunch of set screws.

By the time the eastern horizon was starting to brighten, we had the whole thing ready to go.

"Let's try it out," I said. "See if it'll fire."

The battery was already connected, so all I had to do was pull the ignition wires and touch the hot lead to the starter circuit. The motor groaned but didn't even move. I tried again. Still nothing.

"Oh, man," Emmit said. "Don't tell me . . ."

"Hold on, hold on." I tried a third time. Still nothing.

"Wait," Sean said, pointing at the wire cage around the propeller. "That wire got bashed in somehow and it's jamming the propeller."

Emmit took a stick and whaled on the wire cage a couple times. "That ought to do it."

"Step back." I touched the wires again. This time the engine coughed, spit some fire and smoke. And the propeller began to turn.

We all cheered and high-fived each other.

Then I shut it off.

"What?" Sean said. "Dude, let's roll!"

I shook my head. "We need to get Mike and Farhad and Randall."

"We don't have time," Sean said nervously.

"It'll just take a minute," I said. "We're all in this together."

Sean shook his head uneasily.

"Come on, he's right," Emmit said. "It wouldn't be right to leave them."

"Well, hurry!" Sean said. "We only have twenty minutes before PT. If we're not there, Coach Bell's gonna start looking for us. I mean somebody might have heard the engine and be on the way here right now."

"We'll have to take that chance," I said. "You guys wait here. If I'm not back in fifteen minutes, leave without me."

Emmit and Sean looked at each other.

I turned and ran back through the woods, heading toward campus.

Two minutes later I was inside our dorm room.

"Wake up!" I said.

"Shut up," Mike said. "I'm trying to sleep."

"We got the boat ready to go," I said.

Mike sat up, eyes widening. "You serious?"

I nodded.

"Damn!" He started shaking Farhad and Randall, waking them up.

"I got one more thing to do," I said.

"What?" Mike said.

"It'll just take a minute," I said. "I'll meet you guys back at the boat."

Randall and Farhad were sitting up now, rubbing their eyes.

I started to climb back out the window.

"Hey!" It was Mike.

I turned, looked at him, one foot hanging out the window.

"Are you about to do something stupid, Oz?"

"What?" I said.

His eyes narrowed.

I headed immediately toward Camryn's house. I hadn't told the other guys, but I wanted to bring Camryn along. Knowing what Mrs. Kinnear and Mr. Shugrue had done back in Idaho, I figured her life was in danger. As I drew closer, I saw a big banner hanging from the front of the administration building. WELCOME, PARENTS!

Then I noticed the light at the top of the roof gable of the Kinnears' house was lit. Dr. Kinnear's office. Was he still awake? Or had the light just been left on?

I slid the passkey into the lock, turned it, began sneaking up the creaky stairs. I couldn't hear Mrs. Kinnear snoring. Did that mean anything? Was she awake? I needed to go slowly so as not to make lots of noise on the stairs. But the problem was, I didn't have time to mess around. PT was in less than fifteen minutes. If we weren't in the boat and gone by then, they'd start searching for us.

The last step creaked amazingly loudly. To me it sounded like a gun going off. I froze, stood there for what seemed like forever. Fortunately nobody inside the house seemed to hear it though.

I got to Camryn's door, pushed it open, went inside.

"Oz?" It was Camryn's voice, whispering. "Is that you?"

"Yeah," I said.

"I heard you were in the Silent Room."

"Yeah."

"How did you get out?"

"Look, there's no time for that," I said. "Something bad is about to happen. You need to come with me."

She flipped on her bedside light, sat up. "What—?"

"Like I told you earlier, today is Parents Day. I think your stepmother is going to be leaving tomorrow with a lot of people's money. When she does, there's a chance she's going to bury everybody who could testify against her to the police."

Camryn seemed confused. "But—"

"There's no time. We've got a boat. We're getting off the island. You need to come with us."

"You really think Gwen would kill me?"

"She might."

"But then . . . Daddy's in danger, too."

"Look—"

"Oz!" she said. "We have to take him, too!"

My heart sank. It was true. Her father was probably in more danger than anybody else. But how were we going to get a man in a wheelchair all the way to the boat? It would be hard enough even getting him out of the house without Mrs. Kinnear noticing.

I didn't know what to do.

"Oz!" Camryn grabbed my arm, her fingernails digging into my skin. "I can't leave him."

"Alright . . ." I said.

"I'll get dressed," she said. Then she wrinkled her nose at me flirtatiously. "You don't even have to turn around if you don't want to."

I didn't.

It was kind of a weird feeling seeing her naked. You imagine things like that for a long time and then when it really happens—I don't know—it's like it seems totally normal. And totally not. Both at the same time.

"Let's go!" she whispered.

We went out into the hallway, tiptoed down to Dr. Kinnear's room. Camryn opened the door, looked in, then shook her head and pointed at the ceiling. I took that to mean that he was up in his office in the attic. That's probably why I'd seen the light on.

I followed Camryn up the stairs and we walked into Dr. Kinnear's office. The light was on and Dr. Kinnear was sitting at his desk typing into his computer. He turned and looked at us curiously.

"Oswald?" he said. "Isn't that it?"

"You have to come with us," I said. "You're in danger."

He had a crooked smile on his face, like he was tolerating some kind of dumb gag. "It's five o'clock in the morning," he said. "I'd have thought you'd wait until later in the day for pranks."

Camryn shook her head. "Dad," she said, "Oz has found out some real scary stuff about Gwen. Gwen and Mr. Shugrue."

Dr. Kinnear's face got harder. "Young man, I don't know what kind of joke this is supposed to be, but—"

"Dad!" Camryn hissed. "Keep your voice down! She'll hear us."

"Sir," I said. "This is no joke. Your wife's real name is Alexandra Felder. She's a con woman. She stole over two million dollars from a camp for sick kids out in Idaho. And it looks like she killed the man who ran the camp."

Dr. Kinnear just stared at me.

"Dad, she's been drugging you," Camryn chimed in. "I found the pills! Haven't you noticed that you've been feeling better for the past couple days? It's because I took the drug out of the pills and replaced it with cornstarch."

Camryn's father put his good hand up to his face, started rubbing his forehead.

"Dr. Kinnear," I said, "it's now or never. We have a boat. We can get you off the island. But if you don't come now . . ."

Dr. Kinnear looked around the room like he was confused. I saw his eyes resting on the shelf where all the books he had written were lined up. There must have been fifteen of them. He reached up and touched them. Suddenly his face fell. "You know, I knew she was too good to be true, somehow. A woman that beautiful would never fall for a man like me. A cripple. A bedridden invalid . . ." He took a deep breath. "All that I've worked for. Everything that I've . . ."

"Dad," Camryn said, "we have to go now. We have to find their boat."

Dr. Kinnear's eyes squinted at me for a moment. He seemed very focused all of a sudden. "Can you carry me down the stairs?" he said.

"I think so."

"Good. Camryn, you take my wheelchair. Oswald will carry me."

I went to him and leaned over to pick him up. He was heavier than I expected. As I was struggling to get him out of the chair, my arm hit the shelf behind him and books spilled all over the floor. They made a lot of noise.

We stopped moving, listened. I couldn't hear anything.

"Here, I'll put them up," I said. As soon as I said it, I realized how dumb it was. Why was I worrying about picking up books at a time like this? But before I could stop myself, I had leaned over to grab the books.

Only, when I looked down at them, I realized there was something strange about them. The pages were blank.

I frowned, stared for a moment, picked one up. The cover said, *Dynamics of Childhood Development* by William F. X. Kinnear IV, Ph.D. I flipped through it. Totally blank. I picked up another one. *Fundamentals of Development Neurochemistry* by William F. X. Kinnear IV, Ph.D. There was nothing in it either. Blank page after blank page. I looked up at Dr. Kinnear, my brow furrowing. I had this weird feeling, like something was really wrong. But I couldn't figure out what it was.

Dr. Kinnear looked at me expressionlessly. For a moment he seemed completely blank. And then suddenly his entire face changed. It was as though his skin had suddenly gone hard, like armor.

I started backing away from him.

The man who had supposedly not gotten out of his wheelchair for years rose slowly to his feet.

"Well, Oz," he said, "looks like we got a little situation, don't we?" His voice was different now. Stronger. Harder. Colder. With just the slightest hint of a foreign accent.

And that's when it finally hit me. There had been *three* people who had been suspected in the disappearance of Albert Parker out in Idaho. Alexandra and Abel Felder. And a third man. A man with a funny name, Memluk Sezer. At the time, I'd wondered what kind of name that was.

"Memluk Sezer?" I said. "Is that your real name?"

He smiled, showing off all his teeth. "Hardly matters, does it?"

Then he reached inside his desk, pulled out a gun.

"Camryn, don't let him out the door," he said.

I turned and looked at her. I felt something wash over me—a sense of embarrassment and disappointment and fear all mixed up together. At first I couldn't believe it. But then I knew: she had fooled me and used me this whole time. Camryn was looking at me with this odd little smile on her face. She shrugged. "Sorry, Oz," she said. "Nothing personal. It's just business."

"Are you even his daughter?" I said.

She shrugged. "Like he said—it hardly matters, does it?"

I felt like such a dumbass. She had been manipulating me this whole time. God! No wonder she'd practically thrown herself at me. I was just money to her.

Dr. Kinnear gestured impatiently with the gun. "Cam, we need to find these other kids, stop that boat from leaving."

"Forget it," I said.

Dr. Kinnear raised his pistol and shot me.

It felt like I'd just been clipped by a wicked football. I looked down, saw a red spot in my side about two inches below my ribs.

"Hey, Oz," he said, smiling. "We feeling a little more compliant right about now?"

I just kept staring at the red spot.

"Oh, for Pete's sake, snap out of it," Dr. Kinnear said. "It's just a flesh wound. Nothing fatal about it, trust me." He came around the desk, jabbed the gun in my face. "But believe me, kiddo, you step out of line again and the next one's gonna be right in the center of your chest. Now let's go."

Camryn opened the door, not meeting my eye. I walked

out, holding on to the place where I'd been shot. Truthfully it didn't hurt all that much. But I just felt really queasy and shaky, like I might faint or something.

I walked down the stairs, and Gwen Kinnear—or Alexandra Felder or whatever her real name was—was coming out of the bedroom. She wore sweatpants and a very tight T-shirt that said LA LAKERS BALL GIRL on it. And she was carrying a huge pistol. "What the hell is going on?" she snapped.

"Oz here managed to get out of the Silent Room," Dr. Kinnear said. "Apparently he and his little buddies found a boat and they're planning to escape."

Mrs. Kinnear started swearing like a trooper. "Well, go stop them!" she said finally.

"Hey, genius," Camryn said to her. "What the hell does it look like we're doing?"

"You want me to slap the snot out of you?" Mrs. Kinnear said.

"You two shut up!" Dr. Kinnear said. "It's time to focus. Gwen, go get Bell. Cam and I will take Mr. Smarty-Pants here down to the boat and fix our little problem. Cam, grab the shotgun, and let's go."

"Dude," Cam said angrily, "I did not sign on for mass murder."

"Hey, fine," Dr. Kinnear said. "Did you sign on for spending the next twenty years of your life in the penitentiary?"

Cam didn't say anything.

"Yeah, didn't think so, sweet cheeks," Dr. Kinnear said. "Get the shotgun. Now."

. . .

We walked through the woods, the sun just starting to come up. I heard the bugle blow for reveille.

When we reached the boat, Dr. Kinnear strode out into the middle of the little clearing, pushing me in front of him. The guys had gotten the boat into the water and were all sitting on the deck. They stared at us, trying to figure out what was going on.

"Dr. Kinnear is one of them," I said.

Everybody's face fell.

"Dude, I knew this was a bad idea," Randall said.

"Shut up!" Emmit said.

"Off the boat!" Dr. Kinnear snapped his fingers. "C'mon, c'mon, c'mon. Last guy in the boat, I'm shooting in the head."

Everybody was off the boat in about half a second. Everybody except Mike. He still had the same vague expression on his face that he'd had since getting out of the Silent Room. He just climbed slowly down and splashed through the water toward the land like he didn't really care about anything.

"Shoot him," Dr. Kinnear said to Camryn.

She didn't do anything.

Mike just kept splashing along, finally making it out of the water.

"I said shoot him!"

"You do it," Camryn said.

Mike just kept walking toward us in that slow, retarded way, one hand dangling loosely at his side, like somebody who was paralyzed on one side of his body.

Dr. Kinnear shook his head sharply like he couldn't believe what a wimp Camryn was, then raised his gun.

At that exact moment Mike's face changed and the hand that had been hanging loosely at his side snapped upward. I guess he'd been faking. I could see that he had been holding a big wrench all this time. His hand came up and then he chucked the wrench at Dr. Kinnear as hard as he could.

The wrench caught Dr. Kinnear dead in the center of his face. His gun went off with a sharp bang, then he stepped backward, clutching at his nose.

Without a single moment's thought, I jumped on top of him, wrenched the gun out of his hand, and then did a picture-perfect fake arm drag into a fireman's carry—just exactly like Don Guidry had taught me. Then I turned Dr. Kinnear over and smashed his face into the ground. He went limp as a dishrag.

I had a funny thought: Don Guidry would have been proud of me.

When I stood up, Emmit had the shotgun in his hand and Mike was holding Dr. Kinnear's pistol.

He started kicking Dr. Kinnear's limp body. "Go ahead, scumbag!" Mike yelled. "Put me in the Silent Room again. Huh? Huh? You think you can break me down!" He was yelling and screaming and kicking, tears running down his face.

Randall and Farhad had to grab him and drag him off.

It took a couple minutes to get Mike calmed down.

"Hey," I said. "What happened to Camryn?"

We looked around. She was gone.

Emmit pointed at the ground. There were blood drops in the leaves. "Is that yours?" he said.

I shook my head. "No. I wasn't standing over there."

"Dr. Kinnear must have shot her when his gun went off."

Sean pointed into the woods. "She went that way."

Emmit walked a few feet farther in the direction Sean was pointing. "Yeah. There's more blood."

"Then leave her," I said sharply.

"So are we getting out of here?" Randall said.

Mike had calmed down a little. "No way," he said. "I'm going to get that bitch."

I looked at the other guys. "If we leave on the boat, Mrs. Kinnear's gonna figure out what happened and then she'll ditch," I said. "She'll totally get away."

"So?"

"With our money."

Farhad and Emmit looked at each other. "You make a good point," Emmit said.

"Sean, you and Farhad tie up Dr. Kinnear," I said. "The rest of us will go call the police."

We hustled back to the campus and up to the Kinnears' house.

"You think Mrs. Kinnear is here?" Emmit said.

"One way to find out," I said. Then I kicked the door in. I suppose I probably could have just turned the handle and walked in. But it made me feel better smashing the lock and seeing the pieces fly all over Mrs. Kinnear's precious white rug.

"Let's check the house," I said. "I'll start in the attic. You guys check down here."

I ran up two flights of stairs as fast as I could.

I found Mrs. Kinnear in Dr. Kinnear's office, pecking away at the computer and talking into a headset. Her big revolver was sitting on the desk about six inches away from her hand.

"I'm transferring all the funds into the account in Switzerland," she was saying into the phone as I barged into the room. "From there I'll convert it to zero coupon bonds and then we can—" She looked up in surprise at me. "Abel," she said into the phone, "I'll call you back."

I had my gun pointed at her head.

She eyed her pistol.

"Don't even think about it," I said.

Her fingers were still pecking away furiously at the keys.

"Stop typing!" I yelled.

But she just kept typing, her fingers flying.

"Stop!"

And—just like that—she did. Then she laced her fingers together across her chest, leaned back, and smiled. "All done," she said sweetly.

I reached across the desk, jerked the monitor around so I could see it. Across the top of the screen were the words: *Chase Manhattan Bank Online.* In the middle of the screen was a message that read:

WIRE TRANSFER COMPLETE
TOTAL FUNDS TRANSFERRED: $6,674,211.97

"What happened to Dr. Kinnear?" she said.

"Is that *our* money?" I said.

She laughed brightly, stood up. "Not anymore."

Then she started walking out the door. I didn't know what to do. I couldn't exactly shoot her in the back.

"Stop her!" I yelled down the stairs.

Emmit and Mike appeared at the bottom of the stairs. I

never saw the gun in her hand, but I heard two quick cracks, and Mike and Emmit dove out of her way. I guess she carried more than one pistol.

She pounded down the stairs and out the front door. I followed at what I hoped was a safe enough distance not to get shot.

Mrs. Kinnear sprinted down the gravel road toward the boat landing.

"She's gonna take the airboat!" Emmit yelled.

"Let's go!" I said.

"I'll go get our boat," Mike yelled. "Y'all follow her."

We sprinted after Mrs. Kinnear. For a lady who was no spring chicken, she ran pretty fast. We got to the boathouse just in time to hear the airboat starting up. I couldn't see Mrs. Kinnear. The big door onto the water rolled up and then the airboat was flying out into the water, kicking up spray behind it.

"Wait!" a woman's voice yelled. "Where are you going?"

That's when I saw that Mrs. Kinnear wasn't on the boat. She was standing on the other side of the boathouse shaking her fist. It was Coach Bell on the airboat. "It's all over, Gwen," he yelled. "I'm splitting!" Then he turned around.

"Come back here, you moron!"

"See ya, wouldn't wanna be ya!" Coach Bell yelled back. Then he turned his back on her and slapped the throttle all the way down. The boat leaped forward.

Mrs. Kinnear started shooting wildly at the boat, screaming and cursing as she fired. She kept screaming until the gun clicked empty. Coach Bell's airboat just kept accelerating across the lake, leaving a long curved wake in the glistening water.

We all just stood there staring as Coach Bell made his escape—me, Emmit, and Mrs. Kinnear. The sound of the motor faded and the airboat got smaller and smaller.

"There's no way off the island," I said. "And guess what? You just used up all your bullets."

Mrs. Kinnear kept staring at the boat, her empty pistol hanging limply in her hand. The airboat was heading toward a small opening on the other side of the lake, a little channel between two islands. As it got closer, the boat kept veering off toward one of the islands, still moving on the same slow arc.

"He's not turning," Emmit said.

Just as he said that, the airboat slammed into the smaller of the two islands. There was a fireball, then a gush of black smoke.

"She must have hit him," Emmit said.

Mrs. Kinnear turned and looked at us for a minute. Her eyes were empty. She didn't look pretty anymore. She looked tired and old, like someone who'd had a really bad day.

After a minute she turned and walked to the end of the dock, heaved the gun out into the water. Then she sat down and let her feet trail in the water, shoes and all.

"I'm gonna go call the police," I said to Emmit. "You stay here. If she moves, shoot her."

I walked back to the administration building with the big WEL-COME, PARENTS! banner, went inside and walked into Mr. Akem-pis's office. "I'm going to use your phone," I said.

"Excuse me, but did I just hear you speak to me without saying sir?" he said.

I pointed Dr. Kinnear's gun at him. "I'm going to use your phone now," I said. "Sir."

He looked at the gun and swallowed. "Okay, Oswald," he said. "That would be fine. The pass code is seven-three-three-nine."

I picked up the phone, dialed the pass code, waited for the dial tone, then called my home number.

Mom answered. I'd never been so glad to hear her voice in my whole life.

"Mom?" I said. "Is Don around?"

"No, why?" she said.

"Good," I said. "Because I have a few things I need to tell you."

And that's how it ended, Dad. Well—almost.

Love,

Oz

thirty

Who knows why people do stuff. When I got back to Virginia, Mom thought I should do some kind of exercise to help rehabilitate myself after getting shot. So I tried out for the wrestling team. Maybe it was the feeling of smashing Dr. Kinnear's face into the ground that did it. I don't know.

To my surprise, I made it all the way to the state tournament. Unfortunately I lost in the quarter-finals to this kid from Winchester who looked like he'd been shaving since he was about ten. But still—for a ninth-grader, I did pretty well. I guess it was true: Don Guidry really was a great wrestling coach.

Not that he was coaching me during the season, of course. They arrested him two days after I got home. Mom filed for divorce that same week, and now he's in jail. They found a signed contract between him and Martin Shugrue in a safe deposit box he'd rented at a bank. Mr. Kinnear and Mr. Shugrue had promised him 20 percent of whatever they got if he could figure out a way to get me sent to the Briarwood School. In fact, the Kinnears had given Don this whole booklet on how to make a high-school kid look bad. And he'd pretty much done it all.

The FBI also arrested Martin Shugrue. He's being tried for murder in Idaho. Dr. and Mrs. Kinnear (their real names turned out to be Evelyn and Denny Foster, and they were actually brother and sister) are facing charges for murder and fraud and all kinds of stuff down in Georgia. I'm supposed to testify against them next month. I'm kind of looking forward to it.

The one bummer is, they never found the money. My whole trust fund? Gone. Which is not that big a deal, I guess. I mean I never even knew I had it in the first place—so where's the loss?

They never found Camryn back in the woods. They found Mr. Edson, though. The bullet the police found in his head matched a gun found in Mr. Pardee's house. It also matched a bullet found inside the skeleton we found under the airboat. It turned out that the Briarwood School had been started by a real person named Dr. William Kinnear. He wasn't a famous child psychologist or anything. But still, he was a real guy. Evidently "Mrs. Kinnear" started working at the school, and slowly started taking over. Somewhere along the way the real Dr. Kinnear realized that "Mrs. Kinnear" had plans for him— and that things weren't going to work out well for him. He must have tried to escape the island on his own airboat. Which is when Mr. Pardee apparently caught up with him. That night Mrs. Kinnear fired all the employees of the school. Within a week three new teachers, a new cafeteria lady, and a new Dr. Kinnear showed up.

But back to Camryn.

The police assumed that she bled to death in the forest and then maybe got dragged off by an alligator or something. Eventually the police quit looking for her. But about a month ago I got a box in the mail. It was postmarked from someplace called Vanuatu. I had to look it up. Turns out Vanuatu is this tiny chain of islands somewhere in the Pacific Ocean.

Anyway, taped on the outside of the box was a postcard with this picture of a huge yacht. On the deck of the yacht was this hot babe in a tiny bathing suit blowing a kiss at the camera. The message on the back was written in loopy pink letters:

Dear Oz,

Sorry about everything. I know you probably think I was just pretending to like you so we could scam you. But you know what? I really did have fun with you. It would be cool if I could be like you. Honest and stuff like that. But I guess I'm just not. Anyway. Maybe in another life, ya think?

I kept most of your money. But I kept feeling sorta bad about it, so here's a few bucks just for you. Don't tell your mom. You seem like kind of a serious guy. You should have more fun. Maybe you can buy a dirt bike or something with the money.

It was signed, *You Know Who.*

There was a winking smiley face drawn next to it.

I was thinking, *Get real, Camryn.* Throwing me a couple hundred bucks? What an insult. If she thought I'd spend her measly few hundred dollars just so her conscience would feel better or whatever, she could forget it. I wasn't going to play that game. So I just chucked the box under my bed without opening it.

It stayed under there until yesterday. Mom made me clean up my room, and while I was cleaning, I pulled the box out. For a minute I thought I'd just throw it away out of spite. But then curiosity got the best of me. Well, the truth is, I had been thinking all month, like, yeah, maybe it *would* be cool to get a dirt bike. I'd never even thought about getting one until I got Camryn's card. But now I couldn't get it out of my mind.

So instead of throwing the box away, I opened it. Inside were stacks of bills with little paper bands around them. Hundred-dollar bills. I pulled them all out and counted them. It was seven hundred and sixty thousand dollars.

I put the box under my bed. And I'm keeping it there.

Mom said I could get something special for doing so well on the wrestling team. What do you think, Dad? Should I get a dirt bike?

You son forever,

Oz